PREGNANT MISTRESSES

She's having his baby—
but she longs for his love...

She's been seduced in the bedroom, and now she's pregnant by the man of her dreams. But will she ever have the one thing she wants more than anything—his love?

Don't miss any of the stories in this month's collection!

Price of Passion
Susan Napier

All Night with the Boss
Natalie Anderson

Bedded by a Playboy
Heidi Rice

The Pregnancy Ultimatum
Kate Hardy

We'd love to hear what you think about any of these books. Email us at Presents@hmb.co.uk and find out more information at www.iheartpresents.com

Susan Napier is a former journalist and scriptwriter who turned to writing romance fiction after her two sons were born. She lives in Auckland, New Zealand, with her journalist husband—who generously provides the ongoing inspiration for her fictional heroes—and two temperamental cats, whose curious paws contribute the occasional typographical error when they join her at the keyboard. Born on Valentine's Day, Susan feels it was her destiny to write romances, and, having written more than thirty books for Harlequin, still loves the challenges of working within the genre. She likes writing traditional tales with a twist, and believes that to keep romance alive you have to keep the faith—to believe in love. Not just the romantic kind of love that pervades her books, but the everyday, caring-and-sharing kind of love that builds enduring relationships. Susan's extended family is scattered over the globe—fortunately for her, as she enjoys traveling and seeking out new experiences to fuel her flights of imagination.

Susan loves to hear from readers, and can be contacted by e-mail through the Web site at www.harlequinpresents.com.

PRICE OF PASSION

SUSAN NAPIER

PREGNANT MISTRESSES

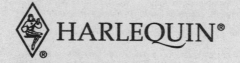

HARLEQUIN®

TORONTO • NEW YORK • LONDON
AMSTERDAM • PARIS • SYDNEY • HAMBURG
STOCKHOLM • ATHENS • TOKYO • MILAN • MADRID
PRAGUE • WARSAW • BUDAPEST • AUCKLAND

ISBN-13: 978-0-373-82061-0
ISBN-10:   0-373-82061-5

PRICE OF PASSION

First North American Publication 2008.

Previously published in the U.K. under the title JUST ONCE.

PRICE
OF PASSION

CHAPTER ONE

'WHAT the hell do you want?'

Kate Crawford kept the polite smile pinned to her lips as she confronted the man who had wrenched his front door open with an impatient snarl.

Framed in the doorway he appeared intimidatingly large, his broad shoulders and muscled chest straining the seams of a well-worn grey tee shirt, scruffy blue jeans encasing his long, power-packed legs. His short-cropped hair stood up in untidy spikes, as if he had been running his large, battered hands through the dark brown thicket, and his deeply tanned face was chiselled into tight angles of hostility.

In spite of his obvious bad temper he was devastatingly handsome, a potent combination of classic male beauty and simmering testosterone. In fact, he looked more like a professional athlete than a best-selling author who spent a good portion of his time sitting at a desk.

'Sorry to disturb you, but I wondered if I could borrow some sugar?' she said, lifting up her empty cup and watching the shock that had rippled across his sculpted features congeal into a shuttered wariness. She was suddenly glad that she was wearing a casual sundress rather than the tailored elegance that was her signature in the city. The last thing she wanted to do was look as if she had dressed to impress. She hadn't even bothered with make-up. After all, she was now officially in holiday mode—the old-fashioned, do-for-yourself, bucket-and-spade, sand-in-the-sandwiches type of holiday, the kind that she had never had as a child.

'I've just moved in next door,' she explained pleasantly, affecting not to notice his stony silence as she waved her free hand towards the beach-front property on the other side of the low, neatly clipped boundary hedge—a small, ageing wooden bungalow, which was dwarfed by the modern, two-storeyed, architect-designed houses that had sprouted up on the two adjoining sections.

'I'm renting the place for a month, and thought I'd brought everything I needed with me, but when I went to make myself a cup of coffee I realised I'd forgotten one of the basics,' she continued with a rueful lift of her slender shoulders. 'I know there's a general store a few kilometres back but, well… I've just spent four hours driving down here from Auckland and I'd rather avoid having to get back in the car for a while. So, if you wouldn't mind tiding me over until tomorrow, I'd appreciate it; and of course I'll pay you back in kind…'

She kept her voice steady, confident that she looked a lot more composed than she felt. Although she was only a little taller than average, the willowy curves, elegant bone structure and haughty facial features that Kate had inherited from her undemonstrative mother helped project an air of cool sophistication and graceful poise, regardless of her inner turmoil. It had never mattered to her mother if the serenity on display was only skin deep. Strong emotions were ruinous to logical thought processes, and therefore to be discouraged. An ambitious criminal lawyer determined to be the youngest woman appointed to New Zealand's judicial bench, Jane

Crawford had wanted her daughter to follow in her footsteps, but Kate had proved a severe disappointment on all fronts. A gentle and imaginative child, she had worked hard at school for only average results and had acquired neither the academic credentials nor the desire to compete with her brilliant, perfectionist mother. In quiet rebellion she had chosen to follow a totally different career path, one that had proved unexpectedly successful and wholly satisfying.

However, at times like this she was thankful for those chilly early lessons in rejection—they had built up her emotional independence and equipped her to face scathing criticism and hurtful rebuffs with a calm resilience that frustrated her opponents.

If she had been relying on the world-famous author to play the gallant hero to her damsel-in-distress routine she had obviously chosen the wrong man, she thought wryly. As a story-teller, his speciality was constructing tough, gritty, anti-heroes who were rude, crude and lethal to know—literally so where female characters were concerned. His creations, much like the man himself, were usually loners, alienated from society by their cynical mistrust of their fellow human beings and stubborn refusal to play by the rules.

Now that he had mastered his initial shock, the gorgeous, dark brown eyes were smouldering at Kate with angry suspicion.

No one was supposed to know where Drake Daniels sequestered himself to write his hugely successful thrillers. He lived mostly out of hotel rooms when he wasn't writing— partying up a storm, generating all the publicity his publisher could wish for on a merry-go-round of talk-shows, book-signings and festivals and special events—ostensibly enjoying his peripatetic lifestyle to the full. But sandwiched between the bouts of public hyperactivity were intervals of total anonymity. Every now and then he would drop out of sight for periods ranging from a few weeks to several months, and each year there would be a new novel on the shelves to delight his fans and confound his critics. To Kate's frustration, a lot of the readily available information about him had turned out to be cleverly placed disinformation. Even his publisher and agent had claimed not to be privy to where in his native New Zealand his private bolt-hole was located. It had taken a great deal of determination, cunning and several strokes of unbelievable luck to finally track him down to the sleepy fishing and farming community of Oyster Beach, tucked away on the east coast of the upper Coromandel Peninsula.

Kate raised her delicately arched brows along with the proffered cup in a gentle hint that she was still waiting for his response, but just as he seemed about to break his stony silence her complacency was shattered by the sound of a throaty feminine voice floating out from the cavernous hall behind him.

'Who is it, darling?'

Kate barely had time to glimpse the tall, voluptuous redhead in a short white towelling robe before the tall masculine figure turned away, blocking her view with his broad shoulders.

'Nobody.' As he spoke he kicked the door closed with his heel, leaving Kate blinking at the honey-gold panels of oiled timber.

For a moment she merely stood, stunned by his insulting dismissal, the blood thundering in her ears. Then she forced herself to walk away, her stomach churning like a washing machine.

Get over it. Move on.

She had done what she came to do. Fired the first shot in her personal little war. There was an old saying that a man surprised was half beaten, so by that measure she could consider herself well on the way to success. But now that she had sacrificed the element of surprise she needed to regroup her defences.

Her flimsy sandals crunched on the crushed-shell path as she retraced her steps along the side of the house with measured strides, resisting the urge to disappear in a cowardly short cut over the low hedge.

The few metres of sandy lawn between the sprawling rear deck of the house and the public beach seemed to take for ever to traverse, but Kate maintained her unhurried pace, acutely conscious of the burnished bank of tinted windows that angled around the back of the house on both upper and lower floors, affording the occupants a clear view of the three-kilometre beach as far as the mouth of the tidal estuary.

Were they watching her retreat, or had they already returned to whatever it was they had been doing before the unexpected interruption? The desire to look back over her shoulder was almost overwhelming, and it took an effort of will for Kate to cling to her feigned air of indifference.

As she reached the lip of the beach a slight, salty breeze riffled through her sun-streaked, caramel-brown hair, sending a few of the long, layered strands feathering across her slender throat. She paused to brush them back, tunnelling her hand under the rest of the silky-straight mass and flipping it free from the textured cotton bodice of her sundress to ripple down between her tense shoulder blades, welcoming the fan of air against the self-conscious burning at the nape of her neck. Her blue eyes narrowed against the splinters of late-afternoon sunlight reflecting off the shifting sea as she tried to gulp in some much-needed oxygen and ease the tightness in her chest. Boats rocked gently at their moorings out in the sheltered bay and, even though it was a glorious spring day and the tide was fully in, the narrow strip of beach was all but empty.

Oyster Beach was only just being discovered by the eager developers who had swallowed up large tracts of coastal land farther south and regurgitated them as fashionable beach resorts. With Auckland only a few hours' drive away, the cove was being promoted as the latest 'unspoiled' getaway for jaded city dwellers. Expensive new holiday houses sporting double garages and *en suite* bathrooms were starting to muscle in on the simple beaches and old-style family homes on their large, flat water-front sections and up in the sheltering hills 'lifestyle blocks' were being shaved off the fringes of productive farmland.

At present the permanent local population was only a few hundred, but that number ballooned to thousands over Christmas and New Year when the schools were out for the long summer break and the pressure on holiday accommodation and facilities was intense. Kate knew that her timing had been serendipitous because November was exam-time at New Zealand high schools and universities. If she had been a few weeks later she would have had little chance of finding anywhere in Oyster Beach for rent, let alone right next door to her quarry. Even the local camping ground was booked out several months in advance for the height of the summer.

At any other time Kate might have been inclined to linger and drink in the tranquillity of the scene in front of her, but at the moment all she could think about was making it back to the sanctuary of her temporary home.

Half-buried boulders wrapped in plastic netting shored up the grass bank at the edge of the beach, protecting the valuable, low-lying land along the foreshore from being eaten away by storm surges. Kate stumbled as she made the short jump down onto the powdery white sand and discovered that her knees were seriously wobbly. Her hands and feet felt cold and heavy at the end of her limbs and her ears had started to ring. She was, she realised with grim awareness of the irony, suffering some of the classic effects of shock—although she had been the one supposedly delivering the jolt!

She stepped back up onto the coarse, springy grass on her side of the hedge and huffed a sigh of relief when her shaky legs proved equal to the task. Moving a little more quickly, she sought the shadow of the creaking verandah and slipped in through the sliding glass door that she had left open to the fresh air.

'Gee, that went really well,' she muttered to the empty house, her fingers whitening around the empty cup as she relived those awful moments of hot humiliation when the door had slammed shut in her face. She had been tempted to storm off vowing never to speak to him again, but she was a mature, twenty-seven-year-old woman, not a sulky, self-absorbed teenager. She had questions to ask and a responsibility to uphold and, as her mother was so fond of telling her, failure was not a viable option!

She put the cup down on the kitchen table and flexed her angry fingers. Realistically speaking, what else had she expected? Drake Daniels had a reputation for freezing off people who became importuning and she had just doorstepped him like a crazed fan, or member of the despised paparazzi. Given his reclusive work habits, she should consider herself lucky that he had opened the door at all.

On the bright side, at least she now had confirmation that she was in the right place at the right time. When she had put her money down for the holiday rental she had been acting as much on gut instinct as on the elusive facts, although her instincts had certainly led her astray in one important aspect: she had not expected to have to cope with a mystery redhead as well as an angry author. Naively, perhaps, she had believed the myth that he crafted his compelling stories in total seclusion.

But that was what she had come here for, wasn't it? To separate the man from the myth? To explore his true character, not just the parts of him that he wanted people to see. Even if it was a truth she found hard to stomach.

She had to get a grip on herself, and not jump to hasty conclusions. Perhaps the woman was a visiting relative, although her research hadn't turned up any mention of living family members.

The slippery coils of nervous tension that had been shifting in her belly all day suddenly tightened, and a rush of saliva into her dry mouth gave Kate just enough warning to make it into the roomy, old-fashioned bathroom before vomiting up the small salad roll that she had made herself eat at a roadside café on the drive down. So much for thinking that it would calm her uneasy digestion!

Kate rinsed the sourness out of her mouth at the basin and dabbed a little refreshing cold water onto her face, dewing her cheeks. Without make-up to emphasis her ghostly silver-blue eyes and narrow mouth she should have looked pallid and un-interesting, but the age-spotted mirror above the basin was re-assuring. One of the few positive legacies she had inherited from her irresponsible, absentee father was a honey-gold complexion that only needed a slight touch of the sun to deepen to a tawny glow. New Zealand was experiencing an unseasonably hot spring, and the meteorologists were predicting more of the same warm, dry weather in the coming weeks, so, if this holiday proved a disastrous mistake in every other way, at least she could return home with a tan that would be the envy of her work-bound housemates, Kate thought wryly.

She flicked her layered fringe aside from its central parting, smoothing it down from her temples to rest alongside the high cheekbones that gave her pale eyes their faintly feline tilt. She accepted that she wasn't beautiful, like her glacial blonde mother, but her sharply etched features were nicely symmetrical, and some men found her unusual eye colour attractive rather than off-putting. Her smile was her secret weapon; when genuine it bestowed a warmth that vanquished the natural aloofness of her expression. She practised it now, to give her wavering spirits a cheerful boost. *If you look confident, you'll act confident,* was another of her mother's bracing maxims, along with aggressive creed, *Don't get mad, get even!*

Purged of her energy-sapping queasiness, Kate suddenly found herself feeling peckish. She fossicked amongst the fresh supplies she had unloaded into the fridge and ate a pottle of yoghurt and some hummus and rice crackers while she waited at the bench for the electric kettle to boil. As she tried to keep her mind from fretting over her next move her gaze swept around the clean but shabby, open-plan kitchen, a far cry from the upscale, central Auckland town house she shared with her friend Sara, and Sara's cousin Josh. The appliances here were all basic models, functional rather than stylish, probably installed when the house was built. The green clocked wallpaper, faded Formica bench and patterned vinyl flooring looked original, too, but what would have seemed highly trendy three decades ago were now sadly dated. She had barely given herself time to unpack before she had trotted out on her abortive begging expedition, but her impression was that the whole place could do with a facelift. The three-bedroom weatherboard house was well-maintained but there was no sign of any attempt at expansion or renovation over the years, and Kate guessed that its present owner had inherited or bought it with the intention of keeping it as a landbank.

The kettle burbled and Kate occupied herself with the mundane task of making a cup of tea. She discarded the sodden tea bag in the sink and added a splash of milk, stirring it in with unnecessary force as her thoughts returned to the complicated tangle her life had become. Choices that had once seemed clear and simple were now fraught with danger, she thought, staring out the kitchen window at the gnarled po-hutukawa tree whose grey-green leaves blocked out the concrete palace that was in the final stages of completion on the other side of the chain-link fence. She hoped that she wasn't about to get strangled in the web of deceit she had been busily weaving.

She raised the steaming cup to her lips for her first sip when a sudden, intangible sizzle of tension in the air made her stiffen. She jerked around, her heart leaping up into her throat as she realised she was no longer alone.

Standing silently in the arched opening between the kitchen and the living room, looking no more friendly than he had a few minutes earlier, was Drake Daniels.

She hoped he put her little choke of dismay down to the hot tea that had spilled onto her fingers. 'What are you doing in here?' she demanded, switching hands to shake off the burning droplets, disgusted to hear that her voice was high and breathless rather than cool and clipped.

'The door was open,' he said, jerking his head in the direction of the verandah. 'I took it to mean that you were expecting me to follow you…'

'It's open because the house is hot and stuffy,' she snapped. She knew she should play it cool, but the sarcastic words came spilling from her lips before she could stop them: 'What the hell do you want?'

His dark eyes glinted. He placed a small plastic container down on the Formica table, centring it with a mocking precision. 'I brought you the sugar you said you needed.'

'Oh.' Kate hugged her tea defensively to her chest as she wrestled with her conscience. 'Thank you,' she said begrudgingly, knowing full well that his meekness was a sham.

Sure enough, as soon as she had humbled herself, he unsheathed his sword.

'So, tell me: are you going to leave when you find out you're wasting your time here? Or is it going to take men in white coats and a restraining order to get rid of you?

'Are you stalking me?'

CHAPTER TWO

'STALKING you?' Kate widened her eyes in amused disbelief. 'You do fancy yourself, don't you?'

Her teasing tone made Drake's mouth thin. 'Stop playing games, Katherine,' he growled. 'How did you find me?'

She sipped her tea and mused on the question. 'I've always found you to be borderline paranoiac, and now it looks like you've inched over the line. Maybe the men in white coats should be coming for you…'

'Very witty—and very evasive.'

She might have known that he'd notice. Words were his business, his strength and his talent…interpreting nuances and assigning subtle layers of meaning to every line of dialogue and paragraph of prose. He would tie her up in verbal knots if she let him. Her best chance was to make simple statements that could be neither proved nor disproved, and then just stick to her guns. Or better still, say nothing at all.

'You're surely not going to claim that it's just pure coincidence that you turned up on my doorstep?' he accused, taking an aggressive stance, legs astride, hands fisting on his hips, a poster-boy for one of his disaffected heroes. 'What's going on, Katherine?'

A tremor of weakness shimmered through her bones. *Oh, if*

only you knew! She looked into his moody countenance and felt the familiar, powerfully seductive tug of physical attraction that was the source of all her current turmoil. She still found it amazing that such a bold, passionate and charismatic man had reacted with such intensity to her ordinary, unremarkable self That it had also taken him by surprise was evident from his hypersensitivity to any hint of possessiveness, and his thinly veiled restlessness whenever they had been together for any length of time. Sophistication had been the name of the game, and for a while she had actually carried it off.

She caught herself up before she could begin to wallow in bittersweet memories, her determination hardening. Oh, no, she wasn't going to let herself fall back into that trap! She was no longer that woman—willing to pander to his genius at the expense of her own needs and goals.

'What's going on is that I'm taking a long-overdue holiday,' she said firmly. 'I've accrued so much extra leave over the past two years that my boss was forced to point out a clause in my contract that says I have until next month to use it or lose it—'

'Marcus?' he interrupted sharply, latching onto the notion that his New Zealand publisher was involved. His eyes kindled with fury at the treachery. 'Enright sent you to find me?'

'Nobody sent me to find you—Marcus has no idea where I am,' she insisted with perfect truth. Her reputation as a dedicated employee who could always be relied upon to work above and beyond the call of duty to support good client liaisons had taken a knock with her abrupt decision to take all the accumulated weeks owing on such short notice, and it had dived even further when she had rejected Marcus's belated offer of a compensatory bonus if she sacrificed the accrual. Enright Media was a very tightly run ship, and it had entailed a lot of fast juggling of favours to get others to take on her responsibilities as well as their own while she was away, but as a researcher she was in a good position to know where the bodies were buried, and how and on whom to apply pressure. A disgruntled Marcus had been forced to concede that he had no legal grounds for insisting she break up her holiday allowance into smaller units, particularly as it meant she would be on deck over Christmas, when staff with young families were clamouring to jump ship.

'I told you, I'm on a holiday. That's when normal people take a break from their workaday lives to rest, travel or zonk out on a beach somewhere.'

'And you expect me to believe that of all the holiday homes in all the beach resorts in all the world, you walk into this one?' he demanded, his deep, velvet-smooth voice steeped in sarcasm.

The paraphrase of the famous line from *Casablanca* struck a painful chord. It had been Kate's ability to recognise quotes from old movies and obscure film noir classics that had captured his attention two years ago, when they had met at one of Marcus' champagne-drenched book-launch parties. They had spent the early part of the evening trading one-liners, Drake's fierce competitiveness challenged by her phenomenal memory for trivia and cool capacity to carry a bluff. Their feuding banter had become increasingly provocative as the night had worn on and Kate had shocked everyone, herself included, by leaving on his arm.

'Coincidences do happen,' she pointed out, relaxing deliberately back against the bench and taking another sip of her tea.

His handsome face rearranged itself into sharp angles of contempt. 'If I tried to use that tired old cliché in a book it would be laughed off the shelves.'

'Which is why they say that truth is stranger than fiction,' she said lightly, regarding him over the rim of the chunky mug. For once she almost felt in control of the relationship as she watched him vibrate with frustration. She was aware of a repressed violence in his nature, but for all his physicality she had never felt threatened by his considerable strength. At thirty-three, he had the maturity and experience to handle his inner demons. Whenever he exploded, it was with clever words rather than crude muscle.

'The strange truth being that less than four weeks after I leave Auckland you "just happen" to choose Oyster Beach for a sudden holiday and then you "just happen" to rent the place next door to mine?'

'Well, gee, I don't usually bother to check out the ownership of neighbouring properties wherever I go, to make sure I'm not inadvertently going to intrude on your precious privacy,' she said, matching him for sarcasm.

His eyes narrowed as he pounced on the perceived slip. 'Then how do you know I'm the owner?'

'The rabid territorialism you're displaying is a dead giveaway,' she said drily. 'Given your reclusive writing habits and erratic timetable, I doubt that you'd feel comfortable working anywhere but your own space. Someplace where you can come and go at will without attracting notice. And it's not as if there's a big choice of long-term rentals if you want something right on the beach…or so the travel agent told me,' she added swiftly.

'So how did you find out about this one?' He jerked his beard-roughened jaw at their surroundings. 'Internet? Newspaper ad?'

She almost agreed before she saw the potential trap. For all she knew the rental had never been actively advertised.

'Serendipity?' She smiled limpidly. 'I read a magazine story about some people who camp at Oyster Beach every Christmas, and then asked around. I am a researcher, you know.'

His jaw tightened. 'And something of an actress, too. You didn't even show a blink of surprise when I opened my door; almost as if you were expecting to see me. Yet you appeared not to recognise me.'

'I was shocked,' she said truthfully. The little electric pulses that zipped through her veins every time she saw him had intensified rather than faded with time. Her hyper-awareness was simultaneously exciting and inhibiting.

'So you just went ahead and trotted out your cheerful little spiel as blandly as if I was someone you'd never met before rather than the man you've been sleeping with for the past two years.'

Colour touched her haughty cheekbones. 'We've never actually slept together,' she corrected him with a crisp exactitude that would have made her mother proud. 'And in the rather awkward circumstances, I thought you would prefer me not to presume on our relationship—'

'Presume?' he echoed incredulously, dropping his hands from his hips. 'Am I really that much of a ogre?'

'Quite frankly, yes,' she punctured his scornful amusement. 'You made it very clear from the very beginning that there are situations and subjects which are strictly off limits between us—'

'I thought that was a mutual arrangement,' he cut in roughly. 'We're two very independent people, and, as I remember it, you're the one who's uncomfortable with the idea of us sleeping together. You never want to stay in my hotel room and you've certainly never invited me to spend the night at your house…'

Behind her back, Kate's hand gripped the sharp edge of the

bench, using the small, cutting pain in her palm as a means of controlling the larger pain. Did he think that she hadn't been aware of the conflicting signals he had given out in those first few weeks? The reckless rush of passion that had precipitated them into an unlikely affair had caught them both off guard. Drake had been between books at the time and making the most of his freedom, and Kate had thought that once he plunged back into his creative cycle his interest would inevitably wane. Not having his experience in the etiquette of conducting casual romantic liaisons, Kate had quietly taken her cues from him. She had seen the way he shied away from gushing, clingy women, had noticed that, although he had a large circle of acquaintances, he had few real friends. He was quick to charm but slow to trust, so she had been very careful never to step over the invisible boundaries that his own behaviour had marked out, or to demand more than she was certain he was prepared to give. The reward for her restraint had been to hold his interest far beyond the usual few months his well-publicised affairs generally lasted. The price of loving Drake Daniels, she had discovered, was not to love him.

She smothered the hot words of protest that tingled on her tongue.

'We're getting off the point—'

'And what is the point?' He cocked his head. 'Oh, yes, that's right—your ridiculous pretence not to know me just now.'

If that wasn't the pot calling the kettle black!

'Maybe I was simply scared you might jump to the arrogant conclusion that I had followed you down here, and accuse me of stalking you! A normal person might shrug it off as just one of life's little amusing quirks, but with you there's no assumption of innocence; no, "Hi, Kate, great to see you—what on earth are you doing in this neck of the woods?" Your paranoid obsession has to build it into some big conspiracy theory centred solely around yourself.'

Temper kicked up a brooding storm in his eyes as he realised she had deftly outmanoeuvred him. 'That was what you meant by "rather awkward circumstances"?'

She hesitated, and lightning comprehension flashed in the storm-dark eyes. 'Ah…I suppose that was a reference to my being with Melissa…?'

Kate cursed herself for giving him the opportunity to torture her with more self-doubts. She was not going to betray the slightest interest in his half-naked companion.

She tilted her chin and gave him a coolly uncomprehending look. 'I meant the fact that I know you hate any interruptions while you're writing—' *Except by the mysterious Melissa,* an evil voice whispered in her ear. 'But if nobody knows where you are, I don't see how they can be expected to know which places to avoid. Perhaps if you were less secretive you might find out that people actually want to avoid you.'

'If you want to avoid me, Katherine, there's an easy solution. Pack up and go elsewhere for your holiday. If the rent isn't refundable I'll reimburse you. Hell, I'll even book you in at a five-star resort somewhere.'

Anywhere but here—he really was desperate to get rid of her! Kate smiled through a thin red veil of rage. 'Thank you, but I've never accepted expensive gifts from you before, and I don't intend to start now. I've already settled in and I'm quite happy with my choice,' she said, safe in the knowledge her bulging suitcases and bags were hidden behind the closed door of the master bedroom, where she had flung them before hurrying next door. She strolled over to sit down at the table with her tea, letting him know that she was unworried by his looming presence. 'I'm looking forward to being able to step out of the house straight onto the beach every day…'

'That's if it stays fine. You're a city girl, you'll get bored here by yourself. There's nothing for you to do if the weather turns— no shops, no cafés or restaurants, no entertainment—'

'Luckily I brought along my own brain,' she said drily, 'an essential accessory for the modern single woman. I'm sure I'll be able to keep myself amused. And I doubt the rest of the local community will be as standoffish as you. Perhaps I'll meet a handsome young fisherman who'll offer to show me the sights,' she added flippantly.

A muscle flickered alongside his compressed mouth. His restless eyes fell to her cup and his dark brows formed a straight line. He sniffed the air like a hound on a fresh scent. 'Is that tea? I thought you said that you were making coffee.'

Her stomach gave a commemorative lurch as another lie come home to roost. 'I changed my mind.'

'I didn't know you drank tea.' He frowned.

'There's a lot you evidently don't know about me,' she pointed out.

'So it would seem.' His gaze shifted to her face and subjected her to a darkly probing look. 'Well, since I brought you the sugar, perhaps you could offer me a cup?'

She barely stopped her mouth from falling open. 'I beg your pardon?'

'But not tea—I'd rather have coffee.' He began to prowl around the kitchen. 'Where are your beans?' He opened the fridge to inspect the shelves. 'God, this all looks depressingly healthy—where's all those lovely, full-fat soft cheeses you're so addicted to…and there's no wine, or stash of chocolate. Prunes? Who takes prunes on holiday? Don't tell me you're on one of those new faddy diets you said your mother is always suggesting you take. What is it this time—South Pacific Colon? Kidney-cleansing Vegan?' He closed the fridge and headed for the pantry.

'Do you mind?' Kate got there first and whipped out the small jar of coffee, pushing it into his chest before he could see the full container of sugar that had been sitting behind it. She shut the cupboard and stood in front of it with folded arms.

'Instant?' He looked pained as he cupped the jar in his big hands. 'What about fresh ground?'

'It's all I've got. Take it or leave it,' she said tartly. At home she had always made sure she had the blend of beans he liked and had taken pains to brew it to his personal taste.

'What in the hell is this? "Decaffeinated?"' he read off the label, as outraged as if he had discovered her keeping a dead body in the pantry.

'It's gentler on the stomach.'

'That's a contradiction in terms; coffee is supposed to kick you like a mule. Is this part of the new diet—some form of aversion therapy?'

'Well, it certainly seems to be working so far,' she muttered, glaring at him in dislike.

His dark head jerked up, eyebrows notching. How could a man who wrote such thrilling, emotionally dense prose be such a blind, insensitive swine? Kate could feel delayed reaction biting deep into her fragile self-control. Next thing he would be wanting her to invite his flame-haired companion over for a bonding drink!

'So I take it you won't be staying for that drink after all?' she said smoothly, sitting back down to her steaming brew.

Still holding her gaze, he unscrewed the lid of the jar, broke the new seal and inhaled the aroma, wrinkling his patrician nose.

'I suppose your tea is decaffeinated too?'

Her hands curled possessively around the mug, drawing it towards her. 'No. But I didn't make a pot, I just used an ordinary tea bag.'

His snobbish palate ignored the blatant discouragement. 'Well, I suppose that'll have to do, then.' She watched in dismay while he snagged a mug from the row of hooks under the cupboards and dropped in one of the tea bags from the open cardboard box on the counter.

'Make yourself at home,' she commented sarcastically as he re-boiled the kettle.

'Thanks. I am,' he said, filling his cup, his quick grin of genuine amusement setting off alarm bells. What had made him so good-humoured all of a sudden?

Kate wished she hadn't made it so obvious that she wanted him to leave, for now it seemed he was going to punish her by lingering.

'Any biscuits?' he asked, returning the milk to the fridge and scooping a teaspoon out of the cutlery drawer.

'No. I thought you were anxious to get back to—' She broke off as he dropped into the chair opposite, his long calves brushing her bare legs under the table, sending a shiver of goose-pimples scooting up her inner thighs. She quickly crossed her legs, swivelling her hips sideways so that she was well away from his unsettling touch, tucking the short, flared skirt neatly under her bottom.

'Back to Melissa?' he completed her question helpfully, heaping sugar into his tea.

Kate's face ached with the strain of not reacting to his casual twist of the knife.

'To your writing,' she said. 'I know you've got deadlines to meet.' She was pleased to see that her hand was rock-steady as she raised her cup to her lips.

'Is that what Marcus told you?'

'Sorry, I don't talk shop while I'm on holiday,' she said coldly. Let him believe that she was here at someone else's behest, if that was the way his mind was tracking. It would take some of the heat off her and, in reality, it was close enough to the truth not to cause her undue guilt.

He blew across his tea, wreathing his dark head in curls of steam: the devil in a domestic setting. 'Then what shall we talk about?' he invited in the deep voice that haunted her dreams.

Her stomach tightened and she lowered her lashes to hide a violent upsurge of emotion. 'What do we usually talk about?'

'Everything.'

And nothing… They never spoke about the disjointed nature of their affair—the weeks of passionate closeness interspersed by months apart, with little or no contact. In a mutual conspiracy of silence they could argue the state of the world, but never the state of their own feelings.

The only place their communications were truly uncensored was in bed, where actions spoke louder than words and their bodies were perfectly attuned to each other's needs. Drake was a generous lover, and Kate found a fierce rapture in his arms that helped carry her through the long, lonely periods of empty yearning.

The things that she ached to say to him were suddenly dammed up behind a thick wall of resentment. He didn't really want to talk, he simply wanted Kate to answer his questions…questions that she didn't yet have answers for herself!

'Nice weather we're having for the time of year,' she said.

'It is indeed…and you're obviously taking full advantage of it,' he agreed, taking up the challenge, his eyes stroking across the honey-coloured skin of her shoulders exposed by the spaghetti straps of her sundress.

Kate was suddenly conscious of the pull of the cotton bodice where it was cut straight across the slope of her breasts, notched in the centre of her cleavage by a V-shaped slit. The flower-splashed, chain-store dress was a comfortable old favourite of hers, despised by her mother for its cheerfully *déclassé* origins. She had never worn overly casual styles in Drake's company, knowing that it was her classic, understated elegance that appealed to his sophisticated tastes, and set her apart from the trend-setting flamboyance of more beautiful rivals for his attention.

She stopped breathing as Drake's gaze drifted down to the sliver of pale skin revealed by the straining V. Nor did she usually go braless when she was with him, preferring the protection and provocation of a lacy bra to enhance her slender curves. She hadn't worn this sundress since last summer, and was suddenly uncomfortably aware of a slight tugging at the side seams, a tightness pressing up under her arms that crowded her breasts forward against the strict cut of the fabric with an unaccustomed boldness. Thankfully the contrasting double-fold of colour that banded the top of the low bodice masked the crushed outline of her painfully sensitive nipples, and allowed her the semblance of indifference as he continued to rudely stare.

Was he making unflattering comparisons…or thinking that she had let herself go? Kate felt faint at the thought. Then she realised that she was still holding her breath and let it out in a little huff of relief, sucking in a fresh supply of oxygen to chase away the dizziness. The sudden reinflation of her lungs caused her breasts to further test their close confinement, and she was mortified to feel a stitch pop.

It wasn't only the dress, it was her own skin she no longer felt comfortable in, she tormented herself. And if he dared to ask if she had gained weight since he had last seen her, he was going to get a faceful of hot tea!

Perhaps he sensed her violent impulse because he rocked back on the hind legs of his chair with a lazy, placating smile, taking a long, leisurely gulp from his mug before resting it on his chest.

'Bright, splashy colours suit you rather well in this setting. That dress makes you look very much the part…' he trailed off suggestively and she obligingly snapped at the bait.

'What part?'

'The young, frivolous holiday-maker out looking for trouble.'

'I've never been frivolous in my life,' said Kate, offended.

He compounded the offence with a mocking grin that creased the sunfolds at the outer corners of his eyes. 'Sorry, perhaps I should have said "carefree"…'

A lot he knew! 'And I'm not "looking for trouble", either,' she added, far less sincerely.

'No? What about your handsome young fisherman?'

'What?' She took a moment to trace the origins of his *non sequitur*. 'That was a joke.'

'Was it?'

His cynical response make her hackles rise. 'You know it was!'

'Do I?' He lowered his chair with a thud and leaned forward on the table, the amusement wiped from his face. 'Because it's not as if there's anything to hold you back from experimenting. We never promised each other total fidelity, did we, Kate?'

Her heart stuttered. Experimenting? Was that what he was doing?

'We never promised each other anything at all,' she forced out evenly. 'But I think at the very least we owe each other a certain degree of respect and consideration.'

'You mean we should be discreet about our indiscretions?' he commented drily, his dark eyes intent on her still face. 'I thought I was…' His shrug encompassed their surroundings. 'A cosy little hideaway "far from the madding crowd's ignoble strife"…how much more careful can a man be?'

Trust Drake to frame a paralysing statement in a poetic quotation, but Kate was inured to his clever verbal games. She battled the crushing pain in her chest to try and work out what he was playing at, because there had to be an angle. He was brutally honest, but rarely deliberately cruel—and never towards Kate. However, she had never breached the unwritten rules of their relationship before…

It was almost as if he wanted her to be furious with him, to rant and rave like a jealous fishwife and insist on being the only woman in his life. Ah, yes…that would give him the perfect excuse to push her away, to end their affair before it threatened to become anything more complicated.

It struck her that a cosy little hideaway was the perfect place to commit a discreet murder!

'Well, you could do your—experimenting—offshore,' she advised, visualising him sinking to the bottom of the bay with an anchor slung around his neck. The satisfying mental picture brought a chill smile to her pale lips.

He shoved away his cup and got restlessly to his feet. She could see that her contrived calm was having the desired effect. 'Aren't you going to finish your tea?'

He looked down at her, his heavy-lidded eyes burning with frustration, his mouth smudged with sullen temper. 'No, thanks. Melissa's probably waiting for me.'

With or without the robe? Kate nodded understandingly. 'Right. You'd better hurry home to reassure her, then. You wouldn't want her to think you were over here firing up your Bunsen burner for an alternative study.'

His eyelids flickered.

'Of course, I'm sure you've already made it clear to her that she's not unique or in any way important in your life. It's always best to be up front about these things, isn't it, Drake?'

Tension pulled the skin tight over the bones of his face. 'We agreed, right at the beginning, that we didn't want any messy emotional scenes—' he grated.

'I'm not the one making a big scene,' Kate cut him off before he said anything irrevocable. She got up and began rinsing out the mugs under the running tap, speaking to him over her cold shoulder. 'I just asked for some sugar, remember? You were the one who came haring after me bristling with ridiculous suspicions and flinging out all sorts of dramatic allegations. You should chill out, Drake, and stop making such a big deal of it. Instead of wasting all that energy worrying about what I'm doing just go back to living your own life. We'll be neighbours for a month, that's all. I'll be as quiet as a mouse…you'll hardly even know I'm around…

'And if you wouldn't mind leaving the rest of that sugar— I think I feel like pancakes for dinner!'

CHAPTER THREE

'MUMMY, look at me!'

The chain on the swing squeaked as Kate swung higher, rocking her small body on the splintery wooden seat to get more speed, stamping her shoes against the hard-packed ground on the down-swing to propel herself up into the wild blue sky.

'Look at me, Mummy!' Her white dress fluttered, her hair spraying out around her head as she rushed through the air, her excited squeals mingling with the squeak and rattle of the chain as she went higher and higher towards the impossible goal—doing a complete loop over the steel support bar. What would happen when she was upside down, she wasn't sure, she only knew that her mother would be proud of her for doing something that only the big boys dared to try.

'Mummy!' She looked for her mummy's proud face but she couldn't see her against the blur of scenery. She suddenly couldn't see any of the other children or mummies and daddies, either—she was all alone in the big, empty park and it was getting dark. There was no one cheering or clapping her brave effort, only the rusty squeak of the chain to accompany her hysterical cry as she realised that she was going too fast and there was no one there to catch her if she fell, or to

stop her from flying off into space and being lost for ever.
'Mummy? *Mummy!*'

Kate jerked into wakefulness, her eyes flying open, her
hands clutching for the dissolving chains and finding only
wrinkled sheets. Morning sunlight filtered in around the dark
curtains, painting bright stripes on the faded wallpaper. The
breath rattled in her chest and the haunting squeak from the
disturbing dream still echoed in her thick head.

She groaned. She didn't need a psychiatrist to interpret the
meaning of *that* little vignette. Her accidental conception
hadn't stopped her mother from ruthlessly applying herself to
her studies and graduating from university with first class
honours. Money had been very tight and, except for during
term-time lectures, there had been none to spare for day-care.
Childish demands for attention had often been greeted with
impatient dismissal or an instruction to play extra quietly.
Before she'd even known what exams were Kate had learned
to dread their approach. Her earliest memory was of lying
under the bed in their cramped, one-roomed apartment whispering stories to herself because Mummy had been studying
for something more important than silly games.

Kate rolled her head on the pillow, trying to rid herself of that
haunting squeak. Except it wasn't coming from inside her head,
she realised, but rising up from the skirting-board where it ran
along behind the bed. And it wasn't a hard, metallic kind of
squeak, either; there was a certain warm *furriness* about it that
suggested some form of rodent. She grimaced at the thought of
mice scampering around the house while she slept. She listened
for the tell-tale scuffling of tiny feet in the woodwork, but the
squeaking was too loud. Far too loud. More like…

Rats!

Kate shot bolt upright in the bed, too late remembering that she should have moved with more care. She grabbed at the package of crackers she had left open on the bedside table and stuffed one into her mouth, but even as she chewed she knew what was coming and, showering a trail of crumbs, she fled into the bathroom.

For the second time in just over twelve hours she inspected the hazed porcelain of the toilet bowl at close quarters.

Kate was never sick. Never. Until a month ago her biological mechanisms had been in perfect sync with her busy lifestyle. Then she had bought that wretched little box in the chemist and her world had gone haywire.

'Damn you, Drake Daniels,' she moaned, in between retches that produced little but burning bile. 'This is all your fault!'

If only it were, she might be able to work up a decent case for hating him. But the truth was that Drake had always been absolutely scrupulous about using birth control. Even though Kate had started on the pill the day after their first time together, he had insisted on using a condom every time they made love. 'No contraception is one hundred per cent perfect,' he had told her bluntly, 'so if we use two methods with optimum effectiveness we lessen the chances of a malfunction.'

Well, Kate was certainly malfunctioning now!

She cleaned up and staggered back to bed.

At least she seemed to have frightened away the mystery squeaker, she thought, lying flat on her back and nibbling cautiously at another cracker, glad to be able to push aside at least one of the problems in her life.

She put a hand on her flat stomach. Here was a problem that wasn't going to go away any time soon. In fact it was growing bigger by the day, although it was still only very tiny—less than half the length of her little finger, according to the books she had read.

How incredible, to have something so physically minuscule yet so all-encompassingly large invading her life! The shock, the dismay, and the sheer, blind panic that had first assailed her when she had stared at the plus sign on the home pregnancy test strip had long since changed to awe.

It was an awe that she could be fairly certain that Drake wouldn't share. He didn't want children. Not ever. He didn't want any physical ties that would compromise his emotional independence. He needed to be alone to write, he had told Kate when they had first met, and nothing and no one took precedence over his writing. As a researcher at Enright Media, Kate was ideally placed to understand the demands of his particular genius. Caught up in the thrill and excitement of being desired by such a fascinating and complex man, she had walked into the affair with her eyes wide open. She had accepted that Drake was not the marrying kind. As their affair had matured into an ongoing relationship she had known that if she objected to his periodic disappearances or acted concerned by his restless comings and goings she would have been rapidly shunted out of his life. So even as she had fallen ever deeper in love with him she had persuaded herself that she was content with the status quo. She was a realist—a practical, self-sufficient, modern woman. She had a fabulous lover, a demanding job with a good salary, and plenty of friends to pal around with when Drake was out of town. No ties suited her just fine. And up until now she had been far too absorbed in her career to even think about having babies…

Dry flakes of cracker stuck in her throat, forming a lump that refused to budge.

Drake had been in Auckland for three whole months prior to taking off to work on his new book—the longest continuous period they had spent together. Kate had dared to hope it

indicated that they were reaching a new level of trust. At first
she had put down her persistent feeling of nausea after he had
left to depression, then to the remnants of a late bout of winter
flu combined with a rush-job involving a biographer who
needed help reconstructing hand-copied notes that a drunken
ex-wife had tried to flush down the toilet. But her weight gain
and the tenderness in her breasts were less easy to dismiss and
when she'd counted back and realised that she was ten days
overdue she had rushed out and bought a test-kit from the
pharmacy. Her hands had been shaking so hard when she'd
used the dipstick that it had taken a while to confirm the earth-
shattering truth.

She was pregnant with Drake Daniels' baby!

She had stopped taking the pill immediately, but it had taken
days for the reality of her situation to sink in, and when it had
she had set about tackling it with her usual pragmatism. She'd
worked out that she was unlikely to be more than a few weeks
pregnant. Unlike her mother, who had married a fellow university student for the sole purpose of exploiting a loophole in the
student allowance scheme, Kate had discovered her accidental
pregnancy early enough to give her a full range of options.

She had made herself carefully consider them all, before
choosing the only one that was ever going to be acceptable to
her woman's heart.

She was *not* going to have an unwanted child.

This baby was already an indivisible part of her, a symbol of
her love, a triumph of hope over pessimism. Her baby had con-
quered almost impossible odds to be conceived; it was now up
to Kate to take over the fight for the best of all possible futures.

She didn't fool herself that Drake was good father material.
But he *was* going to be a father, and she had to decide whether
she wanted him in her baby's life. She had suffered too much

from her own parents' selfishness to want to burden another child with the pain of constant emotional rejection. Until she had made that decision she vowed to tell no one of her condition, her confidence in her ability to be a good mother still too fragile to risk exposing it to the opinions of the wider world.

So she had tracked Drake down to his lair in a desperate attempt to try to establish a better understanding between them before her secret was exposed by her burgeoning body. She had to decide when and how to tell him about the pregnancy, and discover just how much involvement he might want—and she could bear—after the baby was born.

The morning was cool but with the promise of later heat, so Kate pulled on a gauzy skirt and loose tee shirt and caught her hair up into a jaunty pony-tail. She ate a dry piece of toast with a smear of honey and, when she was confident it was going to stay down, indulged the sharp onset of hunger by slicing up a banana and a kiwi fruit into a bowl and spooning over a generous dollop of low-fat vanilla yoghurt. Carrying the bowl in one hand and a cup of green tea in the other, she wandered out to the verandah and perched on the step to eat a leisurely breakfast. The water out in the bay was like shimmering glass, the only movement the gentle ripple of wavelets overturning at the edge of the beach and the swoop and splash of a pied shag arrowing into the water and re-emerging with a squirming fish, which it swallowed with a few flicks of its long neck before flapping off to dry its wings on a rocky outcropping. Licking the last of the yoghurt off her spoon, Kate left the bowl on the step and strolled down to the beach with her green tea. The sand was cool under her bare feet and the crystal-clear water shockingly cold as she paddled out to ankle depth.

As she turned to wade back to shore she saw a lone male

figure standing on the upper deck of the house next door. He was shirtless, his dark mahogany chest smooth and glossy in the sunlight, his tapering torso cut off at the waist by the solid balcony wall, making her wonder if he was fully nude. Drake didn't own any pyjamas and was totally unselfconscious about his body when he wasn't intent on using it for pleasure. The first night they had made love she had been shocked by his lack of inhibitions, and very aware of her own hesitancy in flaunting her nakedness. She had tried to disguise her embarrassment, but to her amazement he had been powerfully aroused by her reticence.

If she hadn't had a few more drinks than usual at the book launch, she probably wouldn't have had the courage to accept Drake's invitation back to his hotel room.

She felt an electrical tingle in her veins at the memory of the weight of his hand on the small of her back as he had unlocked the door to his room. Once inside she had drifted out of his reach, surveying the huge, split-level suite with assumed amusement that had hid a glittering rush of nervous excitement.

'Rather over-the-top for one person, isn't it?' she commented, eyeing the polished black marble pillars, jewelled rugs and luxurious furnishings.

He grinned, tossing his black leather jacket over the back of an antique chair and snagging her evening purse to drop it on the seat. 'Marcus works a great contra-deal for me with the international owner, who's a big a fan of my books.'

'You mention his hotels in your books in exchange for free rooms?' asked Kate dubiously.

'Bite your tongue, sweetheart; I don't play the sap for no one,' he sneered, in a passable Bogie imitation. Given his reputation for laughing criticism to scorn, she was surprised when he added: 'Contrary to what the intellectuals say, I do have some artistic ethics. I don't abuse my readers with sub-liminal advertisements buried in my text. It's an up-front ar-rangement—I do all my press conferences and interviews in his hotels worldwide, and I autograph first editions for him. And the rooms aren't free, I still pay something—but nothing like the rack-rates, so why not enjoy the best on offer? I happen to like the extravagant contrast to the austerity of my other life—my writing life,' he added when she tilted her head quizzically. 'The months when I shrink my world to the size of a keyboard and screen and live like an ascetic. That's why I need to let off steam every time I emerge from my monastic cell—to reduce the risk of a creative meltdown.'

'Writers have a much higher than average occurrence of mood disorders, especially depression,' Kate murmured, won-dering whether she was being naïve to hope she was more than just a convenient escape valve. Not that it mattered. In the space of a few hours the intense euphoria she felt when they had briefly shaken hands during their introduction had devel-oped into a relentless craving; a single, stolen kiss in an empty corner of the crowed room merely confirming her addiction.

'Do we really?' he drawled.

She smiled sheepishly. 'Sorry—occupational hazard for a researcher.'

'You must have a great deal of interesting information squirreled away in odd corners of your brain, waiting to spring out of your subconscious,' he said, his brown eyes narrowing in a fleeting moment of abstraction that made her feel totally invisible.

'Yes, but it's what you do with it that matters,' she said with a wry shrug. 'A lot of it is very esoteric or trivial. Don't confuse memory with intelligence.'

His attention snapped back with uncomfortable intensity. 'What makes you think you're not intelligent?'

She thought of her endless struggles with hated school exams, and her mother's coruscating lecture when Kate had secretly interviewed for a job instead of applying for university.

'Not unintelligent...' That was what had so infuriated her mother. She had viewed Kate's abysmal marks as a wilful act of rebellion. 'Just...um...intellectually unfocused.' This was definitely not the time to be worrying about what her mother might think! 'I suppose I tend to be a Jill of all trades and mistress of none,' she finished lightly.

His smile took on a wickedly sexy smoulder. 'Ah, an intellectual slut...my kind of woman!' he growled.

Kate's nerves skittered at the bizarre sexual imagery induced by his phrase. She didn't know whether to be insulted or flattered.

'I thought we were here to settle an argument about who played Velda in *Kiss Me Deadly*,' she said, glancing at the wide, flat screen hanging on the wall above a sleek, electronic box. 'You said we could watch it here on DVD.'

'I have a better idea,' he said, walking towards her.

'Oh?' Her tongue darted out to moisten her dry lips, heat beginning to flush through her belly and breasts at the fierce expression in his eyes. He hadn't kissed her in the taxi coming over, but he had wanted to, and his restraint had made his desire all the more exciting.

'We both know Maxine Cooper was Velda, so let's forget the movie and I'll show you the real reason I always stay in this particular penthouse...' he purred, taking her hand and beginning to lead her towards the spiral staircase in the corner of the room.

Oh, God, what height of decadence was he about to reveal?

A solid-gold bed with sheets of red silk? A black marble spa pool filled with champagne?

But they kept climbing up past the sprawling main bedroom and stepped out through folded shutters into a magical scene, shaded lights around the high walls illuminating a lush green jungle of plants and a riot of heavily perfumed spring flowers.

'The roof garden…for my exclusive, and very private use…' he said softly, allowing her to walk ahead of him across the dense fan of green grass that divided into winding pathways of creeping groundcover curving around enclosed thickets of soft ferns and spiky palms.

'It's fantastic,' she murmured, her high heels sinking into the turf as she paused by a shrub smothered in starry-white flowers and inhaling the heady night-perfume of Mexican orange blossom.

'That's what I think. Whenever I'm here in town and I start to feel like a victim of my own success, I skip out on the crowds and come up here to mellow out for a while. It's the perfect cure for mood disorders…a little piece of Eden. And now it has its very own Eve…' She heard a faint activating beep and turned to the sound of soft music rising from hidden speakers.

To her shock Drake had shed his footwear and his white silk shirt and was stripping the belt from his dove-grey trousers. At her gasp his hands stilled.

'Have you changed your mind?'

It was on the tip of her tongue to claim that he was assuming way too much. But they would both know it for a lie.

'No, but— I…should we? Out *here?*'

'Why not? It's warm, the grass is soft and the air is sweet, and we're literally closer to heaven than anywhere else in town. But if you're worried we might get buzzed by a police helicopter…' He picked up the remote control he had used to operate the sound system from the glass table beside him and pressed a button. With a low rumble a curved roof of tinted panels extended from the far end of the walled garden and eclipsed the distant stars, finally clicking home against the granite side of the building.

When Kate looked down from this fascinating piece of engineering Drake was stepping out of the last of his clothes, exposing himself without false modesty to her wide-eyed gaze, his large hands, curled into loose fists, hanging quietly at his sides, the angle of the lights painting intriguing shadows in the hollows of his sculpted perfection.

'I want to make love to you now,' he told her with arrogant confidence.

'So I see,' she said shakily, trying to look and sound blasé rather than panic-stricken by his impressive proportions, the thick nest of dark hair in his groin framing a magnificence that would put any one of his highly sexed heroes in the shade.

He shifted restlessly, the muscles bunching in his thighs. 'Aren't you going to reciprocate?' he murmured, nodding at the classic, sleeveless 'little black dress' that she had dressed up for the evening function with cropped blue jacket of oriental design.

Not quite sure how to begin, Kate automatically did what she would normally do at home when preparing for bed, and reached up to pull the pins out of her smooth chignon and let her hair flow like warm caramel through her fingers, shaking her head to fan out the remaining kinks. Then she hesitated, biting her lip as she wondered where she was going to put the pins.

'That's it?' he rasped tightly. 'That's all you're going to do? You're not even going to take off your shoes?'

She thought he was angry, impatient with her nervousness. 'Uh, no, I—' The pins fell from her fingers, spearing silently into the grass around her feet as she realised he wasn't angry at all…far from it! If it was possible, he appeared to be even more aroused than before, prowling towards her stiff-legged, his eyes gleaming black in the muted light, the tension in his voice purely sexual.

'You playing the tease, Katherine?'

'No, of course not!' she denied breathlessly, hypnotised by the fluid play of light and shadow across the shifting planes of his hard body as he continued his hunting prowl across the grass, masculinity personified. As she watched he unfurled a fist, and showed her a palm full of little foil packets. So many? She felt a thrill of exquisite apprehension tingle through her bones, her confidence overpowered by his physiological perfection, her own physical flaws suddenly magnifying themselves in her mind. She instinctively wrapped her jacket across her breasts as he came to a halt, his body crowding hers.

'No? The blushing virgin, then?' he said, tossing the handful of foil to join her scattered hairpins.

She blushed.

'Hardly!'

'You've been around, then?' he said slyly, plucking at the lower edge of the jacket where it poked out below her folded arms.

She tilted her nose up at his deliberate crudity. 'No, I have not "been around",' she sniffed. 'But I have occasionally been in the vicinity,' she admitted with a prim dignity that made his teeth flash white in the darkness.

'Not *my* vicinity, sweetheart, or you wouldn't be acting so cool.'

Cool? She was practically burning up!

'It's just—' She felt something warm—something hard yet invitingly soft—kiss her belly button through her skirt, but she didn't dare look down for fear of losing what little remained of her self-control.

'Just what?' he goaded, 'Just that you're getting cold feet?'

Damn it, if he backed off now she would kill him! She forced her arms to loosen. 'No!'

'No,' he echoed with gritty satisfaction. 'So it must be that you're just too prim and proper to get naked on a first date,' he taunted cockily, his heavy hands settling on her bony hips, his long thumbs massaging the slippery fabric over the smooth skin of her lower belly. 'You've already decided on letting your hair down with me…' he leaned forward to brush his face through the shiny curtain veiling the side of her neck, and inhale the subtle scent of her shampoo mingled with the faintest trace of musky feminine arousal '…mmmm…but the lady obviously wants to be warmed up a little before the main action. You don't want to take them off, ergo you want me to make love to you with your clothes on…'

Her silver eyes widened. 'You can do that?' she blurted foolishly.

Her scepticism made him purr like a sexy tiger.

'Oh, baby, I can do anything you want…'

His big hands slid caressingly down her flanks and slipped under the knee-length hem of her dress, raking up the skirt with his forearms as his hands stroked slowly back up her legs to span her hips.

'Hmm, stockings…that makes things easy…' he discovered on the way up. 'Oh, no…*stay-ups*,' he corrected himself as his fingers found the delicate band that encircled the silky-fine skin of her upper thighs. 'Even easier…'

He sighed when he found the narrow strip of lace drawn

tight over her hip-bones. 'Rippable?' he murmured wistfully, winding one stretchy ribbon around a questing finger, drawing the whisper of satin passing between her legs ravishingly tight against her moistened core.

She squeaked and he laughed, pulling her flush against his scalding nakedness, letting her feel the urgent insistence of his arousal, the rough thicket in his groin catching against her smooth panties. He widened his stance, cupping her bottom as she trembled in a fever of eagerness. 'Never mind, we'll work around them,' he promised in a throaty growl, gathering her tight between his hair-roughened thighs, tipping her off balance as he lifted one of her legs and draped it around his hip. 'I love a challenge…'

He ducked his head and nuzzled aside the jacket to find the outline of her bra against the smooth fabric of the dress, navigating his skilful way to the press of her nipples.

Kate tilted her head back, closing her eyes as she felt the rake of his teeth through the cloth and the simultaneous hot slide of his hardness rocking against her creamy centre, unable to believe this was really happening… She was allowing herself to be ravished by a naked stranger on a rooftop—and she was loving every wicked moment of it!

In a night of glorious firsts she learned that Drake Daniels was very much a man of his word. He delivered on his sensual promise, making love the same way he wrote his books— with fierce concentration and meticulous attention to detail, and a dedication to delivering a climax worthy of his wildly thrilling build-up!

After they had made love several times under the stirring palms they moved inside to the palatial bedroom, and later down to the main part of the suite where they fuelled their sensual excesses from the lavishly stocked bar fridge, and resumed their sexy badinage through a much-interrupted viewing of *Kiss Me Deadly*.

Neither of them slept and in the morning Kate was staggering slightly as she fumbled into her crumpled clothing, aware that having to go home to change was going to make her horribly late for work.

Sitting in the middle of the bed, his lower body swathed in a white sheet, looking very much like a dissipated Greek god, Drake followed her preparations to flee with hooded eyes. His watchful silence made her even more self-conscious.

'I'm never late,' she muttered, stuffing her laddered stockings into her purse and sliding her feet into her grass-flecked heels, uncertain of how to stage-manage a graceful exit.

'This was *not* a good idea…' She meant lingering overlong in his bed, but to her dismay Drake took up her theme.

'Neither of us was thinking—it was nothing to do with choice, it was pure sexual chemistry,' he said abruptly, the dark growth of beard giving his face a saturnine look. He braced himself on one arm, the folds of the sheet pooling in his lap. 'Don't worry, it's like fireworks—dazzling but essentially ephemeral. If we let it alone it'll fizzle out.' The melting brown eyes hardened with cynical resolve. 'But you're right—this can't happen again. It would be a mistake to try and turn it into something that it's not. As it happens, I'm off to LA the day after tomorrow, for an extended book tour across the States…'

Kate disguised her sudden pallor by turning to the full-length wardrobe mirror and raising her arms to fold her hair into a neat self-knot at the nape of her neck in the absence of most of her pins.

He was telling her not to make any plans that included him. They had no future together.

Out of the corner of her eye she could see Drake's partial

reflection past her bent elbows. He was rubbing the centre of his chest with the heel of his hand, as if massaging an ache. He wasn't half as relaxed as he looked, she decided, noting the tension in the set of his head and the fist at the end of his braced arm. Perhaps he expected her to throw a tantrum at his frank rejection of any emotional connection between them, or, worse, to pout and insist on a long-drawn-out discussion of their feelings.

She wasn't going to give him the satisfaction of knowing that she *had* believed they had something special.

Lesson number two in dealing with the unpredictable Drake Daniels:

Never give him what he expects.

She brightened her expression and turned around. 'Right. A mistake. Well…I'll be off, then. See you around. No, don't bother to get up and see me out.' She waved a casually dismissive hand as he made a sharp movement under the sheets. 'I'm quite happy to make my own way. I've been doing it for some years now,' she pointed out with only the barest hint of sarcasm.

'Oh, and if you find yourself in need of another chemistry lesson…feel free to give me a whistle.'

Before he could recognise that vague allusion she had reached the spiral staircase, where she paused to look provocatively back over her shoulder, and hit him square between the eyes with a husky rendition of classic exit-line.

'"You know how to whistle, don't you," Drake?'

It was almost worth the pain of leaving to see his expression, an instant, ungovernable blaze of lust mingled with baffled admiration.

Almost…

CHAPTER FOUR

A MONTH later Kate had answered her cell phone in the early evening to a distinctive, deep velvet voice that had made her heart jump.

'*To Have and Have Not.*'

'Ernest Hemingway,' she murmured automatically, tamping down a dangerous flare of hope.

'I'm flattered, but actually it's Drake Daniels,' he said with typically brazen cheek. Did he really think that picking up exactly where they'd left off was going to make her forget the intervening weeks?

'I know who it is,' she said coolly, her heart still fluttering in her throat. Tucking her personal card in the pocket of his black jacket as she left his hotel room had been a wild gamble she'd thought that she'd lost. Even if he hadn't found it before he'd jetted off to America, he knew where she worked and she was in the phone book

Her eyes darted around the almost empty office and she slumped lower in her seat so her head slipped below the level of her flat-screen display, giving her the illusion of privacy. She had endured a lot of ribbing from colleagues who had seen her leave the party with Drake, especially after her unprecedented late arrival at work the next morning. Luckily, none of them had really believed the fastidious Katherine Crawford capable of getting down-and-dirty on a first date with a serial womaniser, and their interest had rapidly faded on hearing that Drake had left the country.

'I thought you might have forgotten me.'

Fat chance of that, with the reception area plastered with blow-ups of his latest book-jacket! Every morning when she came to work she was greeted at the door by his sexy grin and mocking brown eyes.

'I have an excellent memory for trivia,' she reminded him.

'Ouch!' he said, with the vocal equivalent of a rueful shrug. 'I suppose I should be grateful that it's your passion, then, as well as your profession.'

She found her toes curling inside her delicate pumps. How magnificently he turned his guilt to flattery. 'Most researchers have university degrees—I got lucky when I did a work experience with Enright's just as they were setting up their own PR department,' she found herself telling him. 'Marcus noticed how much I enjoyed reading and how good I was at ferreting out interesting facts for people, and offered me on-the-job training if I stayed. It turned out to be a perfect fit. I like being able to come up with things that surprise and intrigue people.'

'So, I guess you already know that although Hemingway and Faulkner were included in the writing credits for the movie, a lot of the dialogue in *To Have And Have Not* was actually improvised on set.'

'Which goes to show that even great authors don't always get it right,' she shot back, feeling exhilarated and alive again for the first time in a month, but unwilling to let him entirely off the hook. She cupped a hand over her phone as the last of her co-workers in the open-plan office switched off his computer and began loading his briefcase. 'Why are you calling, Drake?'

There was a brief pause during which she visualised him smiling with that irresistible twist of self-derisive arrogance.

'I've forgotten how to whistle,' he drawled. 'I thought you might bring your lips over to remind me.'

Hope burned incandescent, even as she cautioned herself to wariness. Drake was never going to fit into the mould of a conventional lover.

'To New York?' Enright Media subscribed to a multimedia clippings service for all its clients. In spite of her pretence of indifference in front of her colleagues, it had been impossible to resist snooping through the press reports of his trip. He had been last spotted at a famous nightclub in the Big Apple, with the usual phalanx of eager acolytes.

'I'm back in Auckland…at the penthouse.'

She closed her eyes at the powerful memories invoked by his words. 'And obviously at a loose end,' she said wryly.

'I have plenty to do. I'd just rather do it with you,' he said with seductive simplicity. 'There's a party I've been invited to tonight—I thought you might like to go.'

Yes! He wasn't just calling her for a quick sexual fix!

'And afterwards we could come back here…'

Her nipples hardened against her blouse. 'Let me guess— you have a DVD of *To Have And Have Not* for us to watch,' she murmured, giving a weak waggle of her fingers to her colleague as he headed out with a casual reminder of the usual after-work session at a trendy local watering hole.

'Well…that, too, of course…' he said, and she could hear the sexy amusement in his voice. 'Although, tradionalist that I am, I was going to suggest *Casablanca.*'

He would. Romantic but ending in a bittersweet parting—

yes, that would appeal more to Drake's cynical nature than the hopefully upbeat ending for the wise-cracking hero and heroine of *To Have And Have Not*.

'As long as you understand I can't stay the night—I have to start work early tomorrow,' she warned him, drawing her definitive line in the sand. She was never going to risk reliving the painful awkwardness of that first morning-after. She inhaled a deep breath and took the plunge. 'After all, we don't want to make this into something it's not…'

There was an edgy silence. 'You're a devil for matching the quotation to the moment, aren't you?' he said. 'Agreed.' His voice deepened to that spine-tingling drawl that made her feel weak as water. 'I'll just have to make sure that we cram everything in before the witching hour…'

And cram they did. For two years their affair had been a case of feast and famine, with neither side willing to admit to any vulnerability. Had they both been so busy protecting themselves that they had wrecked any chance of building a real relationship?

Kate shaded her forehead with the flat of her hand as she stared up at the lone figure on the balcony. That wary stillness was so characteristic of Drake, the watchful vigilance of a man who had to constantly guard himself against the world. He never spoke about his childhood except in the vaguest of terms, but there had to be something there that had warped his ability to trust…particularly women. He sloughed off praise and criticism with equal ease, using his cynical brand of humour to appear open and gregarious, while in fact revealing little about himself that wasn't already in the public arena.

How long had they been standing there staring at each other, separated by more than just the physical space between them—Drake perched on his high, lonely pedestal, Kate grounded in the ordinary, everyday world he had left behind?

On impulse Kate lifted her hand and waved. For a moment she thought she saw his hand twitch on the shiny aluminium rail as if he was going to wave back, but then she saw Melissa move out from the shade of the house onto the sunlit balcony, and put her hand on his bare arm. He turned to accept the cup she handed him, sliding a brown arm across the back of her dazzling white top as they both retreated inside the house.

At least they weren't having breakfast in bed! thought Kate savagely, letting her hand drop to her somersaulting belly.

'It's OK, little one, I won't let that wicked witch keep your stupid daddy walled up in his ivory tower,' she soothed.

Her green tea had gone cold, and she was tipping it onto the sand when she noticed what was happening to her abandoned breakfast dish.

'Hey!'

She chased up the bank and snatched at the bowl just as it tipped off the side of the step and shattered on a stone that edged the straggly garden.

'Now look what you've done!' she told the big, lolloping dog that peered at her with mournful eyes through its long, matted fringe of mottled grey. It was quite the ugliest animal she had ever seen, looking like a lanky cross between a foolish Afghan and giant poodle on a bad-hair day, with a ridiculous tail that curved lopsidedly over its back in a soggy flag of defiance. It smelled strongly of seaweed and wet wool. 'Give me that!' she said, tugging the spoon out of its gummy mouth, pulling a face at the skein of drool that came along with it.

'Yuk!'

She could have sworn the dog grinned at her before starting to slaver at the pieces of china, rattling them against the stone.

'Don't do that, you'll cut your tongue,' she scolded, pushing at the sandy grey coat. The dog staggered aside and

she was horrified to see that it only had three legs, the right
rear one ending in a woolly stump at its bony hip.

'Oh, you poor thing,' she said, scooping up the broken
bowl and scratching the dog between its floppy ears. It responded with an ecstatic squirming and cheerful caper that
showed her it had well adapted to its handicap.

For all its size it was pathetically scrawny under the shaggy
fur and she wondered if it was a stray, until she saw a glimpse
of black collar buried in the shaggy ruff around its neck.

'Come here and let's see who you are,' she said, but when
she tried to slide her fingers under the black webbing the dog
pranced away, returning to duck and snuffle at her sandy toes,
skittering away again as she squealed with ticklish laughter
at the rough swipe of its tongue.

She put her hands on her hips and tried a stern, 'Heel,' but
the hairy head merely cocked in momentary puzzlement
before it loped over to give a doggy salute to a stunted shrub
at the corner of the house, a performance greatly facilitated
by not having to cock a leg. Then, with a loud 'wuff' that made
her jump, it lunged at the ventilating grate in the base of the
house, its claws rattling against the concrete blocks, and Kate
remembered the rats.

'I don't suppose you're available for a job as a hired
assassin?' she murmured above the excited whines, knowing
that her tender heart would never want even a rat to die
anything but a humane death.

But her three-legged visitor had already revealed a sad
lack of interest in gainful employment, giving one final bark
as it dashed off to investigate a screech of scavenging seagulls
fighting over stolen booty further along the beach.

After wrapping up the fragments of china in newspaper and
making a note of the breakage for the rental agent, Kate did

the rest of her unpacking before deciding the sun was high enough in the sky to be suitable for basking.

She changed into her new bikini, quite modest in terms of coverage but in a vibrant, eye-catching purple piped with lime green that the shop-assistant had assured her would make heads turn. One in particular, she hoped. Since there was a slight breeze she draped herself in the matching see-through, lime-green sun wrap that had cost even more than the exorbitant bikini.

Dragging the light, powdered-aluminium sun-lounger from the 'games cupboard' in the garage out onto the back lawn, Kate unfolded it and positioned it carefully to take advantage of the sun's rays, while making sure it was angled in full view of next door's wrap-around windows. She had originally intended to go down onto the beach, but decided that she would be more visible on the elevated flat of the section.

Stashing a drink bottle where it would be in the shade of her body, along with her sunscreen and a few emergency crackers wrapped in a paper towel, Kate spread a thick beach towel over the woven plastic bed of the lounger and adjusted the back to a comfortable angle. Then she settled down, sliding her sunglasses onto her nose and plopping her purple straw hat on her head. Hefting the glossy library book she had brought with her, she propped it open across her hips.

She would have liked to have read one of the instructional baby books or pregnancy manuals she had hidden away in the bottom of her suitcase, but that would have been a rather obvious give-away, even to an insensitive jackass who was too busy breaking hearts to recognise a good woman when he had her cradled in the palm of his hand…

Kate leafed to page one.

'Simon Macmillan traded in blood and diamonds.'

She had read Drake Daniels' first novel more than once before, but then she had been reading for pleasure—and pride. Now she was reading for research. All authors put something of their real selves into their books. Somewhere in these pages were traces of the man she was trying to understand. Perhaps the skilled researcher in her would be able to sort out some sober facts from the thrilling fiction.

If not, well…she knew it would be a cracking good read, and Mac would turn out to be an undercover good guy who destroyed a dirty deal in conflict diamonds while losing his double-crossing rebel girlfriend to treachery and torture.

Psychological subtext: women are not safe to trust.

At first Kate twitched and shifted and was uncomfortably conscious of her exposed position, but gradually she became engrossed in the familiar story and forgot about ulterior motives, or that she was not supposed to be reading for sheer kicks.

Roused from her trance when her legs began to tingle with warmth, she got up and lowered the back of the lounger so that she could lie down on her stomach, placing the book flat in front on the grass and propping her chin in her hands, wriggling her hips to flatten out the slight sag in the plastic that had been hollowed out by her bottom. Occasionally a midge would perform a crazy loop-the-loop across her field of vision or an annoying fly trickle across the back of her leg, but eventually the drugging combination of sun and sea and weeks of nervous tension took their toll, and before Mac had even kissed his deadly African princess for the first time Kate had drifted off to a light doze, her nose buried in the crook of her elbow.

She was disturbed by a chill shadow across her upper body and surreptitiously wiped the drool that had gathered at the corner of her sleep-slackened mouth on her arm before she lifted her head to smile at her visitor. Shades of that ramshackle dog!

All her cleverly rehearsed phrases zipped out of her head, her smile lingering as a polite rictus when she saw that the figure looming over her was not the tarnished hero of her life but his deadly Titian princess, dressed neck-to-toe in white. Although the hair was more carroty than artistic auburn, decided Kate in an inward yowl, and the lady was definitely pushing thirty, at the very least. That alabaster brow was positively botoxical, and those luscious lips—that *had* to be collagen!

'Hi,' Kate said wittily, pushing the comforting shield of her sunglasses up her nose, while simultaneously trying to untwist the wrap that had got trapped under her side as she tried to gracefully roll over on the uncooperative sun-lounger. The aluminium frame made an ominous creaking sound as her elbow slipped through a gap in the webbing, but she finally managed to wrestle herself free and sit up in reasonable dignity.

'We haven't met, have we? I'm Katherine Crawford.'

She held out her hand. Politeness, she had learned from her lethally charming mother, could be very empowering.

'Melissa Jayson,' came the clipped reply and some minuscule part of Kate relaxed. *Not* Melissa Daniels, then. She crossed one nightmare scenario off her list.

The jade-green eyes that went with the brilliant hair glittered like glass as the politely proffered hand was rudely ignored.

'I don't know what you think you're doing here, but why don't you just get out and leave him alone?'

'I *beg* your pardon?' Kate said, sitting bolt upright, Lady Bracknell in a bathing suit.

'He doesn't *want* you following him. He comes to Oyster Beach to get *away* from the smothering attention of people like you. You can't possibly understand his needs. Give him some space, why don't you?'

'Let me guess, you and Drake are graduates from the same

school of etiquette?' said Kate drily, when she had got over the sting of the lightning attack.

Under the silk top the over-inflated bosom heaved, revealing a gap between the scalloped hem and the low-rise white jeans, and a strip of winter-pale skin sporting the sparkle of an impressive navel ring. Diamonds, no less…probably from Sierra Leone, thought Kate darkly.

Thinking of navels made her think of her baby and she pleated the folds of her wrap over her tummy. By her calculations she was barely two months along, and the books said it would be another two before her baby bulge began to show, but even now she felt a responsibility to shield her son or daughter from negative experiences in the womb.

'Drake and I have known each other since before *you* were around,' the other woman flung at her. She smiled, but only the muscles around her mouth moved. 'He's told me all about you, but you have no idea what he and I are to each other, do you?'

Kate's hormones staged a dangerous mood swing. On the other hand, perhaps it would be good to communicate some fighting spirit from Mama!

'What are you, his mistress or his muse?' she dared to ask bluntly. 'Because I know you can't be both—Drake doesn't trust women enough to allow any of them dominance in more than one compartment of his life.'

'You don't know him as well as you think you do,' came the contemptuous reply. 'You may think you're special but you're really no different from any of his other groupies. You like sharing the limelight with a famous author and helping him spend his money, but you have no idea what it takes for him to create his works. Why don't you stop distracting him and let him get on with his writing—?'

'While you ply him with cups of coffee and mop the

creative sweat from his brow?' said Kate, watching the green eyes flicker and the collagen lips flatten. '*Am* I distracting him?' she added innocently. 'I've only been here one day. If *I'm* a distraction, why aren't you?'

She regretted the rhetorical tag when it was rewarded by a nasty little smile. Melissa looked down, manicured red fingernails flicking an invisible speck off the pristine white jeans. 'Let's just say that Drake has a particular need that only I can fulfil for him. And we keep each other *extremely* well satisfied between the sheets…'

Kate's hand, tucked in her lap, balled into a fist. *This one's for you, kid!*

'Let's not say that. Let's try and be discreet and respectful of each other's feelings, and not start an undignified cat-fight in public.' Her quiet voice stepped up a decibel. She was used to being a mediator in arguments, not an instigator. Confrontation was not her style, but she had witnessed from the cradle how it worked. 'Otherwise I might be tempted to say you're a grade-A, gold-plated bitch who thinks she has the right to run roughshod over other people to get what she wants. But this isn't about you or what you want. Your shame-and-blame tactics aren't going to make me run away with my tail between my legs. I wonder if Drake knows you've snuck over to try and bully me out of his life?'

The redhead stiffened, her elbows tucking into her sides, her jaw clenching as she half turned away, her white sandals acquiring a freckle of dust from the dry grass. 'I suppose you're going to run crying to him telling tales!'

Kate blinked, suspicion curdling in her sour stomach at the subtle body language.

'*Does* he know?' she asked sharply.

'He has been a victim of a stalker before, you know. She

wrote him hundreds of letters—a pathetic woman who thought five minutes of conversation and his personal autograph to her in the flyleaf of a book meant they were soul mates.'

She *hadn't* known, but the evasive reply had the red flags snapping briskly. 'How tragic. I've never even sent Drake a postcard, but if I get an overwhelming urge to buy stamps in bulk I'll be sure and check myself into a facility. Now, if you wouldn't mind moving out of my light, I'm trying to get a suntan.'

'You—'

'Melissa?'

The older woman spun around and saw Drake stepping around the end of the hedge. She immediately walked jerkily back the way she'd come, the two of them exchanging a terse word as they passed each other on the grass without stopping.

Kate took a long pull from her drink bottle and stood up as he came to a halt at the end of the sun lounger. He wore the same disreputable blue jeans that he had worn the day before, with battered workman's boots and a checked shirt with the sleeves rolled up. The decadent, city-dwelling Drake Daniels who wore expensive designer-casual with careless flair was nowhere in sight. Until you looked into his cynical eyes—then the rumpled, down-home, easygoing country-boy was revealed to be the sham. Or perhaps the double life he lived had actually split him off into two distinct personalities. In which case, both of them were in the doghouse with Kate!

She took off her sunglasses to blister him with her naked scorn. 'Next time do your own dirty work.'

'I beg your pardon?' His Lady Bracknell wasn't a patch on hers, she thought.

'Either you sent her over, or you primed her to go off in my direction,' she accused.

He tipped his head down, scowling. 'What did she tell you?'

She gave him a brittle smile. 'That you were fantastic in bed, but since I knew that already the conversation sort of stalled out.'

A trace of discomfort shifted in the dark eyes. 'Kate—'

She didn't want his pity, or his remorse. 'Oh, don't ruin the callous, two-timing image she sketched out so vividly. Just be grateful that I know you don't really believe I'm a bunny-boiling psychotic, or you wouldn't have let your trash-talking girlfriend come within a mile of me. My own father is mooching his life away on a dot in the Pacific because he couldn't handle the responsibility of a relationship with me. You needn't worry that I'm the type to slit my wrists just because a man I respected turns out to be a self-absorbed idiot and coward to boot—'

His face paled, eyes burning in their sockets. 'Don't even say it!' he said harshly, grabbing her arm and jerking her into silence. 'Look, if Melissa went too far, I'm sorry—she thought she was helping...'

'Helping herself to you,' she joked warily, easing her arm out of his painful grip as he seemed to go into physical lockdown.

He looked sick as he watched her massage the blood back into the pale streaks his strong fingers had left on her forearm. She had hormones to blame for her disruptive urges; what made his behaviour so strangely contradictory? For a moment she had had a brief awareness of his potential emotional depths, and realised for the first time that perhaps this journey was going to be more painful for him than it was for her.

In the midst of her own turmoil she felt an irresistible urge to make him smile, to banish that disquieting bleakness from his eyes.

'Gee, and to think Oyster Beach came across as such a pleasant little backwater when I was planning this holiday,' she mused. 'Who knew it would be such a hotbed of passion and intrigue? Inspiration must bite you at every turn—lucky you have your best writing-boots on.'

His mouth twitched, his eyes falling automatically to his feet, which unfortunately brought the book she had been reading into his purview. Face up on the grass, the cover blared its author's first mega-seller in its third reprint. With seven books published in the last six years, in a multitude of languages, each successive blockbuster had guaranteed a surge in new sales for his backlist.

His mouth relaxed into a knowing grin. 'Been reduced to finding your thrills vicariously these days, have you, Kate?' He bent to pick it up, and frowned when he turned it to read the classification code on the spine. 'You got this from a *library?*'

'Don't say it as if it's a dirty word, libraries are wonderful. They're one of the foundations of civilisation—'

'I thought you said you *had* all my books,' he interrupted her, staring broodingly at his younger image on the back cover. 'You work for the publisher, for God's sake. Bloody hell, you could have asked me if you wanted a copy! What happened to the one you had?'

He looked so annoyed that she wasn't going to tell him that her own Drake Danielses were far too precious to her to risk taking to the beach. Better to lose or damage a library book than one of her own first editions, all of which had his slashing signature on the title page, thanks to Marcus' practice of asking every one of his authors for a dozen signed copies to distribute around the office.

'First novels often aren't worth keeping. They're too disappointing when comparing them with an author's later, more refined techniques at work,' she murmured glibly.

For a glorious moment she thought he was going to fall for

it. At least the healthy colour had returned to his face, she thought as he teetered on the edge of an explosion. Then he caught himself.

'Why, Kate, you never complained about my lack of refinement before,' he said, arranging the placement of the book back in her hands so that she had two pairs of identical brown eyes drilling her with their sexy mockery. 'In fact, I thought you liked it. I certainly don't ever recall you saying you found my technical skills disappointing.'

'I know how sensitive you artists are to criticism,' she said acidly, and this time he did laugh out loud.

They both knew his professional ego was bulletproof. He made no secret of the fact his formal schooling had been spotty and at eighteen he had been working as a labourer to save enough money to begin years of travelling. He had worked his passage from port to port around the world on short-haul cargo ships, stopping off to do unskilled labour wherever he could pick up a job, living and working in dangerous environments because they always paid the best money. Curious and observant, he had kept journals throughout his travels, using them as the basis of his first novel. After it had been snapped up for publication he had continued to write because he had stumbled on the purpose of his life. He'd discovered that he had a natural talent for tapping into the popular imagination of millions of people from all cultures and all walks of life, an instinctive gift for words that could make grown men weep and ladies brawl.

'If this is a library book, you must be expecting to be back in Auckland fairly soon?' His eyes ran up and over her, but to her chagrin he didn't seem to notice the knockout bikini, partly because she was hugging his book against her chest, but mostly because he was too busy running through his mental checklist.

'Knowing how much your mother's daughter you are when it comes to the letter of the law, I can't see you deliberately flouting the rules and running up a fine, even if it's only a library fine, so maybe you never planned on staying the whole month here after all,' he worked out, with the convoluted logic of a highly creative mind. 'Maybe you expected to be able to do whatever you came here to do fairly quickly, and be back in town in time to return the book.'

Kate could have told him she had far more pressing concerns weighing on her conscience than late library books. 'That's a bit of a stretch, isn't it, even for you? The loan is for three weeks and you can renew at least twice by phone or online—'

He brushed aside her argument, too intrigued by his paranoid fantasy. 'You don't even have a phone connection in the house, let alone wireless coverage, and the cellular signal is erratic at best. Your mind is far too tidy to leave things like that to chance…no, there's got to be something—'

'For goodness' sake, this isn't the middle of the Gobi Desert, Drake,' she cut in with exasperation, not sure whether he was serious, or simply winding her up. With Drake's sardonic sense of humour it was sometimes difficult to tell. 'I *could* just stroll next door and ask to use *your* internet connection. And don't tell me you don't have one, because you email your manuscripts and revisions.'

He folded his arms over his chest, his smooth jaw set at a stubborn angle as he moodily toyed with the suggestion. 'So you could. Maybe that's the whole idea—access to my computer. I told Marcus there was a good reason the first few chapters are late. He knows I'll deliver the goods. Is he throwing the panic switch already just because I'm not an-swering his emails? Did he put the squeeze on you to do him a personal favour?' He snorted. 'Threaten your job if you didn't use your leverage with me to find out what's going on with the new synopsis, and why I haven't sent the partial? Because if he did any of that, you can tell him that he's violated our confidentiality agreement and he can kiss goodbye to any more books from me.'

'What a shame, and you two have been such loyal friends through all these years, and had such a wonderfully successful run together—you've stuck with Enright Media, even though you must have been wooed by every big publisher in the business,' said Kate, her voice dripping with false compassion at his outrageous threat. 'It seems you just can't trust anyone these days, can you?' Then she clapped her hand to her cheek. 'Oh, that's right, I forgot—you never *do* trust anyone, anyway. How nice it must be to have proof that your lack of faith in your friends has been justified.'

He cooled off instantly. 'I haven't proved anything,' he growled defensively.

She gave him an oozing smile, destined to trigger every warning instinct in his wary nature. 'Just out of interest, why *haven't* you sent him the partial?'

He momentarily froze, and then let out a shuddering breath, running his hand over his head, raking his hair into disturbed peaks. 'Hell, Katherine, rub it in, why don't you?'

'Thank you, I will.' She relished the chance to take her revenge. 'If you really believed that farrago of nonsense it's a short step to thinking that Marcus might have introduced me to you at that party two years ago as part of his long-term strategy of betrayal. I could be a mole.'

'I don't think moles go in for sunbathing, and certainly not in purple bikinis,' he murmured, showing that he was not as impervious as she had supposed. 'They're very solitary, dark-loving creatures, with powerful appetites…'

'That sounds familiar. Maybe *you're* the mole,' she suggested.

'With what mission—to betray myself?'

'Well, it would cut out the middle man.'

A flicker of amusement in his eyes indicated a mocking self-awareness—but as usual when their conversation threatened to breach his invisible walls he deflected her attention away from himself. 'At least we've narrowed down the list of possible motives for you being here. The process of elimination will eventually bring us down to the truth.'

'"You can't handle the truth!" The angry quote from *A Few Good Men* floated into her mind and tripped off her tongue before she could stop it.

'Not been around long enough to qualify as a classic yet, Kate, but it was Jack Nicholson playing Colonel Jessep. And he was wrong, wasn't he? Because people are constantly having to adjust to newly revealed truths…it's called *living*…'

'Some people are too busy crying wolf on their friends or looking for reds-under-the-bed to fully engage in living,' she said, suddenly feeling on the brink of tears. She wasn't going to be stampeded into telling him about their baby in a burst of anger at his wilful lack of understanding. 'Or, in your case, perhaps I should say reds-*in*-the-bed!'

In a flutter of iridescent green she turned to flounce back into the house, but was halted as he grabbed a piece of handkerchief hem.

'Melissa's a freelance editor.'

Kate stilled at the revelation, but didn't turn around. After a moment, he spoke again, his voice rusty with reluctance. 'She's worked on nearly all of my books. I pay her to read the manuscripts for me, give me an overview and correct punctuation and grammar before I send them in. Why do you think my manuscripts are so polished when they land up at Enright's?'

Kate turned slowly, tethered by his fistful of green gauze. She had heard that he only ever required the occasional line-edit. 'But doesn't the editorial department usually do all that stuff?'

He hunched his shoulders. 'I don't get a say at who Marcus employs—I don't like people I don't know taking over and changing things. But I had to do something after the nightmare I went through over the editing on the first book. I have a mild form of dyslexia and never paid much attention to formal English at school so I have two strikes against me. But it is *my* story to tell—and I want to give the nit-pickers as little excuse as possible to tinker with my intentions.'

The light bulb went on inside her head. Of course. This was a Drake Daniels she knew very well. He would do everything he could to minimise the exposure of his weaknesses to others. It was all about *control*.

'But you let Melissa tinker,' she said, eaten up with a jealousy that was far more than sexual.

'We go over it together. She's good at what she does. I know she'll fix the technicalities and throw in a few criticisms and leave the final interpretation to me.'

'Does Marcus know?'

'He doesn't need to know.' He shrugged. 'He doesn't care about the process; all he cares about is that I deliver him a saleable book at the end of it.'

Kate stared at him. She shouldn't be so surprised. *Need to know.* He operated his whole life on that basis.

His fist tightened, putting tension on her wrap as he misinterpreted her long look. 'I suppose now you're wondering if she's more a ghost-writer than an editor.'

It had never even occurred to her. Knowing Drake, she would bet that Melissa had a major battle on her hands with every altered comma.

'Actually, I was wondering how long you two have been together.'

'We're not *together*,' he rejected instantly. 'I send her chunks of the book to read and she comes here to work with me on the edit, that's all. It never takes more than a few days.'

'She calls you "Darling".'

'She calls everybody "Darling".' He clenched his teeth. 'Melissa and I have never slept together.'

His statement fell starkly between them. 'But she obviously would like to,' said Kate.

'A lot of women want to sleep with me; that doesn't mean I do,' he snapped impatiently, hitting on a source of increasing agony for Kate.

'Why not? What's to hold you back?' she gouged viciously at the open wound.

'For God's sake, Kate, I'm not interested and Melissa knows it. Nor is she. That was all an act! She makes a mint off her contract with me, she wouldn't ever want to jeopardise it. Apart from anything else she's *married*.'

'That's no barrier these days.'

His head reared up at the splash of acid in her voice. 'It is for me.'

She would concede that. Too many messy complications.

'What if she got a divorce?' prodded Kate.

'I'm not going to sleep with her, Kate, not even to justify your jealousy.'

He was so smug! 'I'm not jealous!'

He flipped his wrist, winnowing the thin fabric, wafting warm air around her bare thighs and midriff. 'You look pretty green to me!'

His sly humour struck her on the raw. 'Green also happens to be associated with harmony, growth and fertility—' She stopped, stricken. He continued to hold on, his eyes alert with sharpening curiosity, and with a little gasp she rotated quickly away in a balletic twirl that shed her gauzy cocoon, leaving him holding an empty snatch of nothing as her bikini-clad figure disappeared into the house, a sharp click of the latch signalling that her tantalising flight was not an invitation to pursue!

CHAPTER FIVE

KATE was still alive in a state of angry embarrassment a few mornings later when she backed her car out of the garage to head down to the wharf and see if any of the fishing boats she had seen coming in were willing to sell some of their catch from the boat.

The anger was mostly with herself for being a wimp. After coming all this way to challenge Drake, she was now ducking and diving to avoid being seen until her chaotic hormones stopped her leaking tears at inappropriate moments, skulking around inside the house with the doors locked, taking long walks up the beach to find a hidden spot in the sand-dunes where she could do her sunbathing, and driving up into the hills to explore the nature trails.

The embarrassment followed a very uncomfortable second encounter with Melissa Jayson at a local roadside vegetable stall, where Kate had paused on one of her carefully timed walks to buy a bunch of leafy green silver beet, a brown bag of crunchy sugar-snap peas and a large head of broccoli. The stall was a little wooden shed at the entrance to a long driveway heading down into the bush along the estuary shore, the method of payment an honesty box with a large, rusting padlock attached. Kate had been fishing in the lightweight fanny-pack clipped around her waist for the coins to post in the slot when the crunch of tyres and whirr of an electric window had made her turn her head.

'Hello,' Melissa Jayson called from the driver's seat on the far side of the late-model station-wagon. She was in a figure-hugging dress with full make-up emphasising her striking features, but this time all Kate could see was the wedding ring prominently displayed on the finger tapping the steering wheel in time to the beat on the stereo. 'Would you like a lift back to the house?'

'No, thanks, I'm going in the other direction. I'm walking for fitness,' Kate said quickly as her coins clinked into the box.

'Are you sure?' Kate could hear her scepticism. It did seem rather unlikely that she would carry a large bouquet of vegetables around to wilt in the hot sun, when the logical thing would have been to buy them on her way back.

'I'm sure.' Was this an olive branch or a prelude to more backbiting? Should she apologise for calling her a Grade-A bitch? According to Drake the poor woman had only been trying to guard her client's back, or protect her investment, even if with questionable vigour.

'Would you like me to at least take the vegies for you? I could put them in our fridge until you've finished your walk.'

Our fridge? It was ridiculous how much that casually possessive little word grated.

'No, thanks. Really, I'll be fine. I haven't got that much further to go.' For all Drake's protestations that there was nothing between them, Kate was still picking up a vibe that suggested a more than simply professional interest on the redhead's part.

'Well, OK, then, if I can't persuade you...'

'No, but thanks for stopping,' she made herself say.

The Other Woman laughed wryly. 'Really? I bet you wished I'd kept on driving—straight on down into the estuary.'

'The thought did cross my mind,' Kate admitted.

'Well, if it's any consolation, darling, Drake was in a furniture-chewing mood when he came back to the house the other day. He practically got out the thumbscrews to find out what we'd said to each other.'

'Did you tell him?'

This time Melissa's laugh was genuine. 'Are you kidding? After he prowled about like a cat on hot bricks when you arrived, moaning that he wasn't going to be able to write a word while you were breathing down his neck, and then acted as if I'd violated one of the ten commandments by telling you? Let him stew! I gather you didn't tell him much, either— just enough to set him marinating in his own juices. Once he's done he might go well with that broccoli.'

Damn! thought Kate as the car roared off. I wanted to keep hating her and now she won't let me. Sharp, pushy, but up front and funny… Kate could see why Drake might find her good to work with.

It was all his fault. If he hadn't primed both women to resent each other with his manipulative behaviour, she and Melissa might even have been friends. But, of course, Drake wouldn't want that to happen, she brooded—the two opposite sides of his life meeting instead of keeping to his rigid lines of demarcation…

And there was still one good reason to resent Melissa, she reminded herself. She was obviously great at her job. Her position with Drake was highly valued and secure, whereas Kate's was already shaking on its flimsy foundations. Drake would have no trouble finding another lover, but first-class private editors were extremely thin on the ground.

Knowing that she was letting her fears for the future paralyse her will put Kate even more out of sorts. Procrastination had the effect of concentrating her mind on safely trivial concerns, like the fact that every time she set foot outside her door the three-legged dog would dash out of nowhere, drool a greeting over her toes, and hang about with a lugubrious expression until she fed it a few biscuits or a bowl of yoghurt. Or the elusive rodent whose phantom squeak was bothering her at odd times of the day, as well as spooking her at night. She had found an old mousetrap pushed to the back of the cupboard under the bench in the kitchen, still baited with a rock-hard lump of old cheese, but it looked a bit flimsy for the task. Judging by the volume of the squeak her unwanted house-guest was not your average house-mouse.

It occurred to her that she could ask Drake if he was any good at rat-catching. Perhaps it would be a face-saving way of re-approaching him, with the added bonus of being genuine, so if he rebuffed her with the name of a local exterminator she would still have gained something. And if he did offer to personally crawl under her house with a torch and a rat-trap, well…this time she would make sure she didn't let her hormones run riot!

Her sudden craving for a nice piece of fish scotched the rat idea by suggesting a more mature approach. They did say the way to a man's heart was through his stomach and according to her reading the waters around Oyster Beach were famous not only for oysters and a teeming variety of fish, but for particularly plump, juicy scallops.

Drake was a sucker for a scallop.

He had always declared his own cooking skills to be rudimentary, and since there was nothing so glamorous as a restaurant in the small community, and she doubted the take-away joint next to the gas station ran to Coquilles St

Jacques, perhaps offering him a feast of his favourite meal made with delicacies fresh off the boat would create the right atmosphere to re-establish communication. If she also had to invite Melissa for the sake of politeness, well…so be it. It might even prove ultimately more informative than just having Drake by himself. After all, it was thanks to Melissa she was now in possession of a few more intriguing facts…about the way Drake worked, about the dyslexia that might very well be inherited by his son or daughter. She was rapidly coming to understand that even if Drake *wasn't* emotionally involved in his baby's birth and upbringing, there were lots of ways in which he would critically influence the child's life.

Arriving back from the wharf with a bulging plastic bag of scallops, kindly dug from their shells by the grizzled fisherman for no extra charge, Kate swung into her driveway. Halfway back into the garage she remembered she would need mushrooms, too, for the Coquilles. She might have to go as far as the store for those, unless there were some available from roadside stalls on the way. She shifted the car into reverse and put an impatient foot on the accelerator. As she shot back down the driveway in a burst of revs she glimpsed a whisk of mottled grey out of the corner of her eye as it scooted behind the car. She instinctively swerved and jammed on her brakes but there was a jarring thud and high-pitched yelp as the rear wheel ran up onto something and bumped down again.

Kate was out of the car and kneeling beside the back tyre within seconds, scraping her hands on the decorative rocks that lined the drive as she braced herself to peer underneath. Wedging the mud-flap against black rubber tread was the ubiquitous three-legged dog, no longer irritating her with its foolish antics but lying lax, and ominously still. Grateful that the wheel wasn't actually resting on the dog, Kate scrambled back into the idling car, and with shaking hands slowly drove it forward until she estimated it was well clear of the fallen victim.

This time when she knelt on the driveway beside the dog, she was relieved to see its side shuddering and its head lift briefly before thumping back onto the rough concrete with an accompanying low whine, the stump of the missing leg twitching pathetically, the ridiculous tail limp and streaked with a dark stain she feared could be blood.

'Oh, God—' Stricken with guilt, she tentatively touched the trembling coat, wary of causing any more damage to broken ribs. 'It's all right,' she said shakily, daring a few, butterfly-light, pats. 'You'll be all right once we get you to the vet… he'll fix you up…'

She knew there was no way she was going to be able to lift the heavy animal into the car by herself, nor did she have any idea if there was a vet anywhere close. Murmuring foolishly to the dog that she'd be back in a moment, she ran around into Drake's paved front yard and hammered violently at his door. It seemed to take an age for him to open it and as soon as he did she gabbled wildly:

'I've hit a dog with my car. I think it might be badly hurt, but I'm not sure. It's just lying there, whimpering, and I don't know who owns it or what to do. Is there a vet around here, or a doctor I could take it to for help?' But in her panic she didn't think to wait for an answer, she was running back, anxious not to leave the dog injured and alone. If it died she didn't want it to die alone.

By the time she got there Drake was beside her, cursing under his breath when he saw the animal, crouching down and running his large hands over the hairy hide, running explorative fingers through the thick pelt, eliciting a feeble flicker of the tip of the foolish tail.

'It was my fault—I mustn't have looked properly,' Kate agonised. 'It ran behind the car when I was backing. Thank God it wasn't a child!' The thought made her feel ill. 'I can't have been going very fast but I think maybe it went under the wheel—'

'Him,' said Drake tersely, cutting off her semi-hysterical spate of words.

'What?'

'It's a "him", not an "it". He's obviously a male,' he said, his face oddly desolate and blank of expression as he gently manipulated each of the three big paws and quieted the broken whines with an indistinct murmur.

'Oh, I wasn't sure…with all that hair,' Kate quavered, grateful to cling to a steadying fact in a sea of wretched uncertainty. 'He's been hanging around ever since I got here, but I don't know where he comes from. Do you think he'll be OK?' she asked anxiously.

'I don't know. I can't feel anything broken but we need to get him to a vet as soon as possible in case he's bleeding internally. There's a clinic about thirty kilometres away, near Whitianga—it covers a big rural area as well as the town, but they always have more than one vet on call.'

Internal bleeding! Kate's stomach twisted as Drake continued, 'The only visible sign of trouble I can see is this graze on his muzzle.' He withdrew his hand from the dog's mouth and turned it over to show her the bright red splodge of blood on his palm. Kate's senses swam and she turned away and was promptly sick on the edge of the grass.

'Sorry…shock,' she mumbled, taking the handkerchief he thrust at her and wiping her mouth.

'You didn't hit your head?' he asked sharply, his face pale and set, his mouth grim.

He looked more shaken than she had ever seen him,

fighting some inward battle for calm, and she realised he must be worrying about concussion. She put her hand over her belly, freshly aware of the fragility of life, and grateful for her habit of caution.

'No, I was wearing my seat belt, of course, and anyway, as I said, I wasn't going that fast—'

He shifted his crouch, leaning forward to slide his arms under the dog's recumbent form, smoothly straightening his legs in order to rise to his full height without jolting. As Kate suspected, the big-boned dog was even heavier than he looked and the strain on Drake's neck and shoulders was clearly visible as he adjusted his unwieldy burden against his chest. Kate winced at the pitiful yelp that the move elicited, and hurried to open the rear door of the car, but Drake was already moving in the opposite direction.

'Where are you going?' she cried, almost tripping as she hastened on his heels.

'He's obviously not going to fit in your car lying down. I have a four-wheel drive with very good suspension—he'll be less likely to be cramped or jostled. Go and get my keys from Melissa, and tell her to call the vet—the number's in the red index on my desk.'

By the time she had breathlessly returned Drake had the dog lying full length on a tartan rug on the wide back seat of his battered grey Land Rover. He grabbed the car keys from her hand and hefted himself up into the front seat.

'Wait!' said Kate, scrabbling at the back door handle as he gunned the ignition.

He frowned impatiently at her through the open window. 'There's no need for you to come. I know where I'm going—'

Kate's shaking hands succeeded in getting the door wrenched open. 'Of course I have to come,' she said, shocked he would think otherwise. 'I injured him; I'm responsible for him. I can't just abandon him for others to look after!'

'Nobody's accusing you of abandoning him. You got help, that's as much as you could do.' He swore. 'Damn it, I don't have time to argue—'

'So stop arguing and start driving,' ordered Kate, climbing in behind him and shutting the door with a snap. She eased herself down on the bench seat by the dog's head and squirmed her way into the seat belt, being careful not to entangle the animal.

'What if something happened on the way?' she pointed out as Drake pulled onto the road. 'You have to concentrate on your driving. The poor thing is probably scared out of its wits as well as being in pain. He could hurt himself again if he starts to panic. He might not be used to travelling in a car.' Her tight voice dropped into a croon. 'Someone's got to be here to hold your paw, don't they, boy?'

The dog was lying on its side, and its panting breath moistened her bare thigh below her khaki shorts. She fondled a floppy ear and brushed the woolly strands of fur away from the single visible eye, which glistened dolefully, making her feel even more guilty. For once she was grateful when he gave her leg a disgustingly gooey swipe.

'Oh! He licked me. Do you think that's a good sign?' she said hopefully.

'Licking you is always a sign that something good's about to happen,' came the mocking response.

Kate's glare drilled into the back of his head above the headrest. 'How can you make jokes at a time like this?'

'What better time to try and deflect thoughts of doom and gloom?' he said harshly. 'Humour in the face of adversity is a very useful human defence mechanism.'

Of course it was, and particularly so for Drake, she realised. The dry wit, flirtatious wordplay and entertaining anecdotes with which he avoided intrusive questions were the perfect distraction from his real feelings. Didn't she do exactly the same thing when trying to shield herself from caring too much?

She looked over at his hands on the wheel, and noticed them shifting with a rapidity and frequency that wasn't necessary for the control of the vehicle. He was fighting frustration, charged with adrenalin-fuelled urgency that he had to control for the sake of driving them safely on the narrow, winding roads.

She felt a movement against her leg, the dog trying valiantly to shift its heavy head into her lap, as if attempting to comfort her with its trusting forgiveness. She squirmed closer so that she could help him lift his grazed muzzle across her thigh.

In between croonings she speculated about his ownership, undeterred by Drake's clipped responses.

'I wonder who owns him. Do you know? A dog with three legs…he must be well-known in the neighbourhood—'

'He certainly strays around—'

Kate was quick to cut him off. 'He's not a stray! Are you, boy?' she soothed the dog. 'He's got a collar, but every time I try to twist it around to look for the tag, he cringes. He has to belong to someone. Someone who doesn't look after you properly, eh, boy? I don't think he can be fed very much, he's always pestering me for titbits—'

'If you bend over him in that purple bikini I can understand why.'

She met his eyes in the rear-vision mirror above the dash. 'Drake! I'm being serious. He always seems to be ravenous.'

'He's obviously a hardened scrounger.' His eyes flicked carelessly back to the road.

'Don't say that; he can hear you!' said Kate, putting a hand over the dog's ear. 'I told you he has a collar. If his owner's not caring properly for him he's got no choice but to scavenge. He can't very well hunt for himself with only three legs.'

'He seems to have managed to track down your bleeding heart.'

She frowned at his apparent callousness. 'His coat seems very messy,' she said, picking out a burr. 'He could do with a brush.'

He lifted his chin to bring the dog into his line of sight. 'Probably been rolling in the dirt. He's a mutt, not a show-pooch.'

'I wonder if he's ever groomed? Owners like that should be shot!'

'I thought you were a proponent of non-violence?' His narrowed eyes met hers for a brief challenge before swerving away again.

'It's just a turn of phrase,' she said impatiently. 'Pet owners have a responsibility.'

'He's more like a nuisance than a pet.'

Now she was truly shocked. 'It's not his fault. He shouldn't be allowed to wander.'

'Maybe he *needs* to roam.'

Kate gritted her teeth at his stubborn refusal to share her sensible concerns. How could she love such a hard-hearted man? And how could such a hard-hearted man ever make room in his petrified organ for the love of a child? She leaned across the dog's head, her tee-shirt tickling its nose into a messy snuffle. 'But it's dangerous—'

'This is the countryside; risks are assessed differently in remote areas,' he said as she quickly leaned back again. 'People here don't keep their dogs penned up.'

'But he could at least be kept in a fenced yard—'

'Oh, for God's sake—get real!' He looked daggers at her in the mirror. 'He hates being shut in. He goes berserk if you try to tie him up or keep him behind the fence; he nearly kills himself trying to get loose.'

Kate's hands stilled their restless stroking, her eyes widening as the certainty hit her like a freight train.

'He belongs to you!'

His eyes whipped back to the road. 'He's a stray.'

It all came together. The shocked curse. The grim examination. Having the vet's phone number handy on his desk. And, most telling of all, the hard carapace of flinty self-control.

'Maybe he was a stray, once. But he's your dog now, isn't he?'

'Nobody wanted a hopeless mongrel like him.' He shrugged. 'He would have been put down.'

She took that as a yes. 'Because he only had three legs?'

'He had all four when he first landed on my doorstep,' he said drily. 'He lost his back leg when he practically shredded it ripping his way through a chain-link dog-fence I put up to keep him "safe".' He glanced back just long enough to see her wince. 'Which of course only made him even more unattractive to your average dog-lover who either wants a purebred or something useful or cute.'

'So when did you adopt him?'

'I didn't adopt him.' He sounded as if she had accused him of an iniquity. The muscles at the back of his neck stiffened. 'The vet says he was probably abused in a confined space as a pup—which makes him very much of an outside dog. I've never owned an animal, but said I'd let him hang around at my place until something could be arranged that didn't involve a lethal injection. That was five years ago, just after I built the house. Unfortunately no one ever answered the ads, and I'm still stuck with him.'

And still deep in denial about it!

He had built the house with the proceeds of that first book, she realised. Prior to that he had been a wanderer, spending his money as he went. But as soon as he'd had the means, he had made a place for himself, and, although he might categorise it purely as a place to write, a temporary refuge, it was more than that—it was *home*. He had been secretly putting down roots.

'What happens to him when you go away?' she asked curiously. 'If he hates being shut up he obviously can't go into a kennel.'

'I usually drop him off with a mate of the vet's, who has a lifestyle block up in the hills. In the shorter term I pay a local to come and live in the house,' he admitted gruffly. In other words he firmly kept a foot in both camps—the dog owner and the rootless wanderer. And, of course, he also had his town mistress on a completely separate string!

'Doesn't he pine?'

'Not noticeably. He likes company but he's not particular. He doesn't like to be owned. Mostly he needs the freedom to come and go.'

He could be talking about himself, thought Kate, struck by the stunning psychological similarity. They both had attachment issues. She had often wondered about Drake's family background, but he had never responded to her tentative comments, and she knew only the vague details—that he had been orphaned as a teenager by the death of his mother, and had no contact with his father. She suspected abuse, but had known better than to ask.

She did have one more question, however, that did urgently require an answer: 'So what's his name?'

'He didn't come with a birth certificate.'

'You must have given him a proper name.'

'Since he never comes when I call him, it seems a bit pointless.'

'So what is it?' She could see he was relishing her frustration at his evasions. She could also see that his hands were more relaxed on the wheel and the muscles in his jaw were no longer clenched. 'Let me guess.' She pretended to think. 'Rumpelstiltskin!'

He almost smiled.

'No? How about Rover? Very appropriate to his nature.'

There was no response from dog or man.

'Spot? Montmorency de Waverley Assortment?'

That got her a human snicker. She raised her eyebrows and he gave in to her persistence, his worried eyes wary as they reflected his surrender.

'Prince.'

'Prince,' she repeated. There was suddenly a huge lump in the middle of her throat. It could have been a mocking appellation, but from his shifty expression she guessed otherwise. It was the wry and wistful choice of a boy for his first dog. Drake had called his shambling, shabby, shock-haired goof 'Prince', and now at least something about the woolly hound would have the dignity that genetics had cruelly denied him.

She looked down to hide the sting of tears. Drake might act as if he had no desire for commitment, but the existence of Prince suggested that at some level he *did* want to establish emotional ties in his life. He may not *choose* to love, but he *could* and *did* love.

And if one love could force its way into his well-guarded heart, why not another?

'I'm very sorry I hurt Prince,' she said quietly. Would he

ever be able to forgive her if she caused the death of his dog? 'I should have been more careful.'

He didn't rush to absolve her with soothing lies, but he did offer her comfort to ease her guilt. 'So should he. He makes a sport of pretending to chase cars. He's been knocked about before. It was an accident, Kate.'

He sounded fatalistic, but Kate knew better. He had simply internalised his fear. 'I hope he's all right.'

'We'll soon find out. The clinic is just up ahead.'

The white-coated vet who came out to greet them with a metal gurney was a tall, thin man about Drake's age, with a long-suffering expression on his bright and humorous face. 'You're lucky I hadn't gone out on rounds yet, Drake. At this rate I should get a royal warrant to stick on my door. What on earth has Prince done to himself now?'

'Not him—me—' Kate began, only to have her explanations pre-empted by Drake's terse account as he lifted the whining dog onto the gurney. The vet's friendly air didn't dilute his brisk professionalism and he kept up his patter as he pushed the gurney through the doors and past the reception desk in the waiting room.

'We'll take him straight through to the surgery and I'll assess whether he needs a scan. But we'll start off with the cheap option.' He cast a smile into Kate's anxious face. 'That's me. Hands and eyes are a vet's most valuable tools.'

'I'll be paying, so I don't care how much it costs,' she blurted. 'Just do everything you can—'

'Don't be ridiculous,' Drake said roughly, stroking the dog's head. 'I can afford any treatment he needs—just send the bill to me as usual, Ken.'

'But—'

'For God's sake, Kate, stop making it such a drama. I don't

need your guilt money!' he snapped as they paused for the vet to open the surgery door.

Kate's hand fell away from the gurney. She knew it was fear making him lash out, but it still hurt to hear him declare he wanted nothing from her, and she had to steady herself against the wall.

'Are you all right?' said the vet, his eyes suddenly sharp on her pale face.

She stared at the name badge pinned to his coat as she fought for composure.

'Ken Cartwright B.V.Sc.' the black lettering said as it moved briefly in and out of focus, making her feel as if she were standing on shifting ground. 'I'm just a little dizzy,' she excused herself.

'She threw up before we left,' added Drake unnecessarily.

Ken's sharp gaze became speculative as it ran over her from head to toe. Oh, God, she hoped that vets didn't have any special instinct for detecting early pregnancy in humans!

'Perhaps you should sit down for a few minutes—Christy!' Ken called out to his receptionist. 'Would you get a glass of water for Kate here, while Drake and I see to Prince?'

'Oh, really, I'm fine…' she murmured, but Ken was already disappearing into his surgery with the gurney, while Drake hesitated outside.

Kate braced herself, but when he frowned it wasn't to issue another rejection. 'Are you sure it's only dizziness? Are you feeling sick again?' He glanced restlessly over his shoulder at the closed door and back at Kate, his eyes black with inner turmoil, clearly torn.

Drake never vacillated. He always knew what his priorities were and was never afraid to make harsh decisions.

'Go,' she urged, freeing him from his agony of choice. 'I

don't need you—Prince does. Go and find out what's happening to your dog.' And when he still hesitated, she gave him a physical push. 'For God's sake, *go*! I have to go to the bathroom, anyway, so there's no point in your hanging around here. Go!'

And having given him the freedom to follow his heart, she went off to find her glass of water and have a short, but deeply satisfying cry in the toilet cubicle, under the beady eyes of six fat hamsters crowded onto the veterinary products calendar on the back of the door.

CHAPTER SIX

IT SEEMED an age, but it probably wasn't much more than twenty minutes before Drake came back out into the waiting area.

Kate took one look at his shuttered expression and dry eyes and her heart sank. His body seemed tautly bunched under the woven cotton shirt and stonewashed jeans, simmering with unexploded tension, his mouth hard enough to chew nails.

Ken Cartwright, who was steering him with a consoling hand on his shoulder, was more relaxed—although he must face this sort of situation fairly often in his professional life.

'Well, that's it. I've done all I can. I think you'd better take this guy home and give him a stiff whiskey.'

He thought alcohol the best way to handle grief? Kate's heart swelled in her chest.

'Oh, Drake,' she said helplessly, sharing his misery, 'I'm so sorry. Your beautiful dog!' She burst into tears and threw her compassionate arms around his neck, burying her wet face in his chest.

His arms came up to clamp around her shaking body, his strong, encircling arms almost muffling out the sound of the vet's next words.

'Beautiful? She surely can't be talking about Prince—his ugly mug would win the booby prize at Crufts!'

Kate stiffened, her head bumping Drake's chin, unable to believe her ears. She could feel the chest under her wet cheek silently vibrating…oh, God, was he actually *crying*?

She turned her head and gave the grinning Ken Cartwright B.V.Sc. a blistering look.

'You call yourself a vet? What kind of thing is that to say to a man who's just lost his dog?'

'Prince is lost? Are those tears of relief?' Ken grinned over her angry head at Drake. 'You should be so lucky!'

Kate's jaw dropped. 'Someone should report you to the—to the—'

'The place where people report vets for making really bad jokes?' he supplied. 'I'm sorry, Kate. But it looks like Drake is going to have that ugly mug around for the fore-seeable future.'

'You mean he's still alive?' She jerked her head back to look up into Drake's face through tangled wet lashes.

'He's more than OK. He's perfect.' The smile he was wearing was even bigger than Ken's. It hadn't been dammed-up grief, but fierce relief that he had been fighting to control when he'd walked out!

'Is he?' she sought professional confirmation from the man she had been vilifying only seconds ago.

'A bouncing box of birds.'

Kate blinked at his cheerful alliteration and pulled her hands from Drake's neck to swipe the wetness from her cheeks. 'But there was blood—'

'Rubbed a bit of skin off his nose, that's all.'

'I felt the bump, I felt the car go over him—'

'No sign of any crushing, or marks on his coat. Are you sure it wasn't something else you ran over?'

'No…at least, there were some rocks along the side of the

driveway…' she faltered, remembering how the steering wheel had seemed to jump out of her hands when she had swerved to try and avoid the dog '…but he was lying there up against the tyre, whimpering and whining—'

'Yes, fancies himself a bit of a Hollywood star, does our Prince. Wouldn't surprise me if you gave him a bit of a nudge and he decided to fall over and ham it up. For all he's skittish he likes attention, especially from a tasty woman.' He winked.

'He travelled all the way here with his head buried in her lap,' said Drake drily.

'Lucky dog!' chuckled Ken, making Kate pinken. 'Here I thought he was some kind of giant schnauzer-cross and he turns out to be a ladies' lap-dog. 'Nuff said!'

Kate suddenly realised she was still snuggled up against Drake, her stomach pressing into the buckle of his jeans, her breasts squashed into the narrow space between their upper bodies. She wedged her elbows against his chest and shoved herself out of his entangling arms—with difficulty because he seemed reluctant to cooperate. Probably because he knew what she was going to say.

'You knew I thought he was dead! And you were laughing at me!' she shouted.

'Not at you, sweetheart—*with* you,' protested Drake, acknowledging his utter defencelessness to the charge.

'You insensitive pig!' She scrubbed again at her cheeks to make sure all trace of her sympathy was gone. Unfortunately, so were her chances of appearing aloof in her displeasure. 'You and that—that…scrofulous hound deserve each other. I bet he was laughing at me too,' she said, remembering the lolling tongue.

'Is she always so volatile?' asked Ken.

Drake's eyes darkened as he looked down at her, curiosity

mingled with a dawning new awareness. Kate tensed, sure he was going to say something witty and suggestive.

'I'm not sure,' he said slowly. 'She's rather difficult to get to know.'

'*I'm* difficult!' Her momentary speechlessness gave the vet time to step in by smoothly suggesting that his assistant had had time to give the dog his antibiotic injection by now.

'I don't think there's any chance of infection to his nose, but I'll give you some antibiotic cream to take with you, Drake, just in case. Come and get Prince and I'll give you a sample box from the surgery.' He smiled at Kate. 'It was nice to meet you, even in this roundabout fashion. The mouth-trap here doesn't give up much, but I won't pretend not to know who you are…we get given lots of gossipy magazines for the waiting room here. I hope this doesn't put you off your visit..?'

He was blatantly fishing, and Kate ignored Drake's restless movement to cruise by the bait. 'Oh, I'm not staying with Drake. I've rented my own house on Oyster Beach…'

'Next door to mine,' Drake chipped in, only to be totally ignored by his so-called friend.

'Oh, really?' The blue eyes twinkled at Kate. 'Ever been out on a racing catamaran?'

'No, she hasn't—she gets seasick in the bath. I thought you were going to get me that prescription? You have a sick tortoise over there who's been waiting long enough.'

'Mmm, he does look a bit green,' said Ken, with a glance at his next patient, clutched to the chest of an old man who looked not unlike a wrinkly tortoise himself.

Kate bit off a gurgle as Drake glared at her. 'You wait here,' he said sternly.

Ken pointed towards the chairs, using the same tone of voice. 'Yes, sit, girl, sit!'

Christy was on the phone and Kate hovered by the desk for a few moments thinking to ask her if she knew anything about rats. But the receptionist seemed to be getting into an argument about a bill, so Kate moved to a discreet distance, inspecting the various posters on the walls.

She was standing in front of a glossy chart showing the life-cycle of the blowfly complete with close-up photographs of the rear ends of maggoty sheep when a gravelly voice said: 'Revolting little devils, aren't they? And fancy having to live in a sheep's bum! Give me a good, old-fashioned, lusty leech any old day.'

Kate turned to find herself the target of a pair of vivid green eyes deep-set in a pale, intense face. For a brief moment she was distracted by the mop of flaming red hair, unpleasantly reminded of the woman who had given her so much cause for discomfort, but then her senses responded to the very male impact of the unshaven chin and sexy mouth, the lazy, white-lidded gaze and the lean, tapering body encased in a black tee shirt and jeans. His face said he was somewhere in his thirties, but the decadent eyes were much, much older.

'Oh, I don't know,' she said, consciously trying to act normal. It was difficult when he looked so fascinated by her own eyes, but perhaps that fathomless gaze was just part of his technique. 'Some maggots have a useful side, too. Like leeches, they're being used medicinally in some hospitals—to help remove dead tissue in and around infected wounds. They're supposedly more effective than surgery because they don't excise any healthy flesh.'

Oh, yes, have a conversation with the man about rotting flesh—very normal, Kate!

He received the lecture in flattering silence, moving around to lean a casual shoulder against the wall. 'I'll never swat a fly again,' he vowed, hand on his heart. 'But I still prefer blood-suckers to scum-suckers. Leeches seem like they might be more fun to hang around with at parties…'

'You would know,' she murmured, and bit her lip, thinking that might have been a bit rude.

His eyelids drooped, his trade-mark, world-weary smile hiking his sensual mouth. 'OK, now we both know that you know who *I* am,' said Steve Marlow, former bad-boy rock-star, now New Zealand's—and one of Hollywood's—most sought-after composer of movie-music. 'Am I allowed to know who *you* are?'

'Kate.'

'Tell me, Kate…' he jacked one black-booted foot over the other as he trotted out one of the most hoary old clichés in the pick-up business '…do you come here often?'

Her heart didn't even miss a beat. 'Only in the maggot season.'

He laughed, his attractively harsh voice projecting off the walls. Shaking his head, he looked around the now-empty waiting room. 'Are you here to pick up an animal?'

'I'm here with a friend.'

'So am I. My nephew's pet rabbit who has been losing some of his rabbity-bits in order not to over-populate his hutch.' He placed his hand on the wall above her head and leaned confidingly closer. 'Has anyone told you what absolutely stunning eyes you have?'

'Yes. *I* have,' said Drake, striding across the floor to slip his hand under Kate's elbow and tug her away, her feet stumbling as Prince blundered eagerly between them to head-butt Steve Marlow in the thigh.

'Ouch! Can't you keep this damned dog of yours under control?'

'I am. He's trained to attack tired, old, talentless has-beens who sleaze around younger women desperately trying to relive their faded days of glory!'

'I still can't believe you said that,' a mortified Kate was repeating as he encouraged Prince to jump up into the back seat of the Land Rover and settle down on his tartan rug. 'You just insulted a Kiwi icon. It's a wonder he didn't punch you in the nose, like he did that music critic backstage at the Oscars!'

'He'd have to pump up those skinny arms first!' sneered Drake, hustling her around to the front passenger door.

Just as she was getting in, Steve Marlow came out of the clinic with a carry-cage, and walked over to a black convertible parked near the door.

He looked across the gravel parking yard at them, and lifted up the cage to show Kate the sluggish white behemoth squatting within. 'Hey, Drake!' he called, in his famously husky voice. 'Are you still on for our usual Friday-night pool session?'

The mocking lilt made Drake stiffen. 'Why wouldn't I be?'

The bright green gaze went pointedly to Kate's sun-burnished head. 'Oh, I don't know…Ken and I just thought you might have found more exciting things to do…'

Drake made a growling sound deep in his chest. 'You and Ken are gossiping old women! I'll be there, with bells on. The both of you can prepare to go down in a screaming heap—*as usual*.'

'What about Kiss Me Kate with the sexy silver eyes—will she be coming, too?'

'She doesn't play pool.' Drake slammed her door with unnecessary force and got behind the wheel.

'She could hold our beers!' The gravelly yell that had sold a million albums degenerated into a burst of coughing as the Land Rover did a sharp turn past him, kicking up a cloud of dust into his face.

Drake pulled his arm back inside the open window and turned onto the black tarmac.

'Did you just make an obscene gesture at him?' said Kate disapprovingly.

'He did it first.'

Sure enough, as she looked out the back window she could see Steve Marlow's black-clad figure extending a crudely upthrust finger at the departing vehicle.

'He looks just like the cover of his breakthrough album,' she laughed.

'Poseur!' snorted Drake.

Kate hid a smile. 'I didn't know you two were friends.'

She held her breath but to her delight he didn't shy away from her obvious curiosity. 'We knew each other for a while as kids. We've kicked around a bit since we met up again several years ago. Why would I boast about it?'

Why indeed? He never gossiped about others, or name-dropped to impress. He didn't have to—he was quite impressive enough on his own account.

'Goodness, Oyster Beach is turning out to be quite the Celebrity Central,' said Kate, settling back in her seat.

'You won't run into Steve at the beach,' said Drake, sounding smug about it. 'He burns like a vampire in the sun. The Marlow family have a holiday place way back in the valley,' he said with deliberate vagueness. 'Steve's only there now and then, in between shuttling back and forth to the UK and the States.'

'I suppose having to protect his skin from the sun is what keeps him looking so boyishly young,' Kate mused, unable to resist feeding his evident irritation.

'More likely a decaying old painting riddled with corruption stashed away in his attic!' he grunted.

'I thought he seemed very nice,' she said demurely.

'*Nice?* He's a fire-born hell-raiser from way back! He's dangerous. Stay away from him.'

As if she had a choice! She knew very well that Steve Marlow had just been idling away a few minutes of his time. It was the arrival of his friend that had truly piqued his interest. And Drake had played right into his hands.

'He's obviously not the same person he was when he was with the band—'

'But he's done it all…booze, fags, tattoos—sex, drugs and rock'n'roll. Who knows what perversions he's into now to give his jaded senses a kick? You can do practically anything you like in Tinseltown. He's not someone you want to know.'

He sounded as pious as a priest. 'I thought you liked him, I thought he was your friend?' she said, bewildered.

He hunched over the wheel. 'I do. He is. That doesn't mean I'd let him date my sister,' he muttered.

Her mind stuttered to a stop as she swivelled in her seat to stare at him. 'You have a *sister*?'

His profile hardened. 'I don't have any family; I was just using the word metaphorically,' he grated. 'We're talking about you.'

She recoiled. 'And you think of me in a *sisterly* way?'

'Of course not—you know what I mean.' He cast her an accusing look. 'You're too good for him.'

'You mean I'm a goody-goody,' she said resentfully. She wound down the window to cool her cheeks in the rushing air. It was true. Becoming Drake's lover was the baddest thing she had ever done, she brooded. Of course, having an illegitimate baby was about to put paid to that goody-goody image for ever!

'Well, I happen to think his music has always been terrific,' she said defiantly. 'Even when he was with Hard Times. They produced some classics of the hard-rock genre—'

'Yeah, and thanks to that he has enough groupies hot on his tail. He doesn't need you drooling over him, too.'

That was the second time in a few days she had been insulted by the same accusation. 'I am not a groupie!'

'No? What is it with you, then? Have you started giving off some pheromone that announces you're available? You never even *notice* other men when you're with me, but all of a sudden you're flirting with everything in pants—first Ken, then Steve—'

'Flirting?' Kate spluttered. 'I was attempting to engage in normal conversation with two men I'd never met before. If there was flirting going on, your friends were the ones doing it. And that was only because you were bristling like a dog around a bone. You're so jealous you can't even see—'

'Jealous!'

She gasped as he suddenly swerved, and pulled into a rest stop carved out of the bush-covered cliff at the side of the road, no longer trusting himself to drive. He yanked on the brake and cut the engine, turning to confront her across the console with a savage face. 'That's rich, coming from *you.*'

She tried to dial back her anger in the face of his, realising that her not-so-innocent prodding had stirred up a hornet's nest, but determined to stand up for her rights. 'Oh, I see— it's all right for you to dangle another woman under my nose and accuse *me* of being jealous, but when the shoe's on the other foot it's a different matter.'

'Don't ever accuse me of being jealous,' he spat at her.

'Why not? It's not a dirty word.'

'It is to me,' he said, so thickly he could hardly get the words out.

'But—*why*?'

He gave her a look of impotent fury. Neither of them heard

Prince whine in the back seat. 'I'm not that person,' he said through his teeth.

'What person?' And when he remained silent, she nudged him: 'A little bit of jealousy is usually considered healthy in a relationship.'

'In a healthy relationship, yes. In an unhealthy relationship it can be dangerous for everyone involved,' he said rawly. 'It can eat a person up from the inside and be hugely destructive.'

She felt a frisson of fear. That sounded very like personal experience talking. 'What do you classify as an unhealthy relationship? Is that what we have?'

He angrily pushed away the past, his eyes hot as they slammed into hers. 'No, of course not, because we know how to control it, we don't let it control us—we're equals.'

'And what if I don't want *control* any more?' she challenged recklessly. 'What if I want something different?'

The heat in his eyes turned molten. 'Is that what the matter is, Kate? Is life getting too tame for you when I'm away? Can't get any satisfaction? The lack of sex making you edgy and restless…sending you out looking for diversions?'

He leaned over, flipped open the clasp of her seat belt and dragged her against his chest, pinning her hips across the central console. 'Well, here's a diversion for you!'

His hot mouth sealed over hers, his hand tunnelling up under her shiny mass of hair to cup the back of her delicate skull, tipping her head to give him deeper access to the moist, satiny cavern. His tongue stabbed, stroked, enticed…the slight roughness of his jaw scraping her chin, his musky male scent teasing her nostrils, filling her with a familiar sense of heady abandonment.

His mouth slid around to her ear, his teeth nipping then sucking suggestively at the tender lobe.

She shuddered, her hands clenching on his shoulders, fingers digging through his shirt into hard muscle, and his hot breath fanned the sensitive nerves behind her ears as he laughed roughly. 'Oh, yes, you like that, don't you? I know all the things that turn you on…' He used his tongue to stroke the delicate little nub of flesh, sending fresh quivers through her body. 'You like the things I do to you, because you know I can give you exactly want you want…'

The hand pressing on the middle of her back moved around to shape her breast through the soft tee shirt, cupping the soft weight and his thumb stroking her stiffening nipple through the intricate lace of her bra as he kissed his way across her throat to tease and play with the dainty lobe of her other ear.

'For instance, I know that when I'm doing this, you're remembering about how it feels when I suckle that other, even more exquisitely sensitive little bud…' he whispered roughly. 'You know the one…the secret one that's tingling right now between your legs, making you long to bite and claw and scream for me, the way you do when we're in bed…'

Kate's hips writhed helplessly against the hard console as she squeezed her thighs together to try and ease the forbidden throb intensified by his taunting words. His hand tightened on her breast, compressing the pleasure into an even greater density, drawing at her thrusting nipple in a rhythmic counterpoint to his softly suckling mouth.

'Drake—' Kate groaned, her hands sliding from his shoulders to the neck of his shirt, lusting for the feel of his bare skin against her seeking fingers.

'Yeah, baby, it's me,' he said, lifting his head to look down into her silver eyes, drowning in blind desire, before breaking open her kiss-stung lips with his teeth to feast once again on her voluptuous surrender. 'Who else could it be? Who else knows how to turn you on so hard, so fast? You can be cool and standoffish with other men, but not with me, never with me…'

It was true, and the fact that he knew it and yet still withheld the essence of himself from her should have been humiliating, but it wasn't, for she could hear the exultation that overlaid the taunting passion in his voice. Something deep and powerful and primitive within him wanted her to be for him, and him alone, regardless of what his private demons were telling him.

A deep rumble tore from his chest, vibrating through her fingertips spread over the warm hollow at the base of his throat, and the big hand holding her head shifted to her shoulder blades, keeping her still as he worked impatiently at the front catch of her bra through the folds of her tee shirt.

Just as Kate felt the plastic clasp give way, they were wrenched from their mutual absorption by a roar and brief, blaring toot.

Kate jerked back, her dazed eyes following Steve Marlow's black convertible as it swept out of sight around the corner.

'Oh, God!' she said, pushing away his hands and fumbling to do up her bra, not half as deft as he at conquering the small clip through the masking material.

'I bet he got an eyeful!' said Drake, with a hint of malicious gratification.

'Did you know he was going to be coming this way?' she paused in her pink-cheeked struggles to ask suspiciously.

'The valley road turn-off is a few kilometres further on, but I didn't plan this, if that's what you're thinking.'

'I wouldn't put it past you.' She frowned.

'Well, I didn't. Which is not to say I'm not pleased he saw us.' He met her glower with a mocking shrug. 'It's a guy thing… Here, let me help you with that…' He put his warm hands up under her tee shirt and boldly drew the cups of her bra together, his fingers brushing her taut nipples a little too often for it to be accidental as he eased the lacy fabric into place around her breasts and neatly snapped the clip into place. 'There,' he said thickly, adjusting her breasts for one final time in their snug cocoon, his hands reluctantly trickling away down her quivering tummy. 'Maybe we should take this into the back seat,' he murmured, watching her black pupils expand even further into the silver irises.

She cast a guilty look behind them, struggling to find a reason to resist his alluring suggestion. 'Prince is there,' she remembered with a relieved gasp, prompting the dog to lift his head at the sound of his name and loose an ear-splitting 'woof'.

'There's plenty of room. He can scrunch up, or hop into the front seat and watch…'

'I don't think so,' she began repressively. Her honey skin became even more flushed under his sultry gaze as she realised he was only teasing. He had never meant her to take his suggestion seriously. She tried to hide her chagrin by adding smoothly, 'He might be traumatised for life.'

'*I* might be traumatised if we don't,' muttered Drake, rolling his hips and tugging at the denim to ease the constricted front of his jeans. To her embarrassment Kate realised that he hadn't even undone his seat belt…she was the one who had been doing all the writhing and squirming.

'I should have remembered you don't like making love where there's any chance of being caught *in flagrante*,' he continued to needle, 'but I thought you said you wanted something different. Now I see you're all talk and no action.' He switched on the engine and put his hand on the automatic gear-shift, shifting it out of park in preparation to pull back out onto the road.

Trust him to reduce her demand to the lowest common denominator—sex. Two could play at that game!

Kate stopped fishing under her bottom for the end of her seat belt and grabbed the collar of his shirt, jerking his head down and around so that she could stretch over and plant a deep, soulful kiss on his unsuspecting lips, using her tongue to glide her way into the slippery recesses of his hot mouth.

At the same time, she ran her flat hand firmly down the front of his shirt to the buckle of his jeans. She felt the tension in his stomach and knew he thought she was going to keep on sliding her hand down until it cupped the bulging denim pushing out the zip. Instead she increased the pressure on her hand and thrust it between the denim band and loose hang of his shirt, reaching into the tight space between jeans and skin at the apex of his strong thighs. She felt an electrifying jolt go through his entire body, his shocked jaw sagging open to her exploring mouth as she fanned her fingers out over the silky distension in his briefs, tracing the rigid tip of his erection, feeling it pulse against her circling thumb.

He groaned, his hips lifting, the lunging twist of his chest towards her engaging the locking mechanism of his seat belt, trapping him at the mercy of her exploring touch. He was about to wrench himself free when she cruelly broke off the kiss.

'What I want different is for *me* to dictate the choices,' she purred. 'And what I choose now is to go home and have a cheese and pickle sandwich for lunch, so—carry on, driver!' And with one last, wicked little tease of his straining manhood she was withdrawing her hand from his pants when another car tooted past, briefly slowing as it drew alongside, this time a big, sturdy, dust-laden four-wheel drive with the personalised number-plate VET KEN.

When Drake had finished cursing a blue streak at her

actions he looked over at Kate, buckled into her seat belt and sitting primly upright looking serenely ahead, her hands folded in her lap.

'You're as red as a poppy,' he discovered.

She could imagine. She could imagine far too much, that was her trouble, she thought, smoothing her hair nervously behind her ear.

'His seat was so high up…do you think he could see what I was doing?' she couldn't help asking.

Drake laughed so hard that Kate refused to speak to him all the way back to Oyster Beach, but it was hard to act cool and dignified when you had been spied with your hand down a man's pants! It didn't seem fair that her foolish attempt at revenge had rebounded so embarrassingly on herself. Or that she had found it so unexpectedly arousing to toy with Drake in that scandalous way on the open roadside. If Kate was hauled up on a charge of public indecency her mother would have fifty fits—and probably recommend hard time in the slammer!

Even Prince seemed to be having a sly laugh at her expense as he punctuated Drake's continuing chuckles with an occasional wuffle, and he added insult to injury when he leapt out of the car at the other end and raced around as if he'd just undergone a day at a leisure spa rather than prompted a mercy dash to the clinic to save his life.

Kate apologised stiffly to Drake for the disruption to his day. 'I hope I haven't put you and Melissa too far behind in your schedule by dragging you away from your writing for so long,' she said, and beat a hasty retreat as his lingering smirk turned to a moody frown.

It wasn't until she'd forced down a cheese and pickle sandwich in order not to make even more of a liar of herself that she remembered the scallops she had left in the front seat of her car.

She went to fetch them and stowed them on the bottom shelf of the fridge. Then, worried they might have already gone off by sitting for more than an hour in the hot sun, she took them out to put them to the sniff test. They seemed fine, but to risk eating spoiled seafood was foolish when any toxic reaction had the potential to hurt her baby. Anyway, she had gone off the idea of a dinner party, she thought as she wrapped the scallops in newspaper and placed them in the rubbish bin outside the kitchen door.

So she was stunned when, later that afternoon, Drake knocked at her door and asked her over for dinner, hastening to add that he wasn't doing the cooking.

'Melissa's going to do scallops—she always insists on doing the cooking when she's here; it's the only way she claims she can get a decent meal,' he said, unknowingly rubbing salt in her wounds.

'I don't think I—'

'It's in the nature of a farewell dinner. Melissa goes back home tomorrow.' The casualness of his words were belied by the sensuous awareness in his eyes. Tomorrow one source of upheaval between them would be gone. Melissa would go back to her husband and Drake would…what? Retreat? Or advance?

'She'd really like you to come,' he said, strolling back to the verandah steps and turning to say, 'And so would I.'

'The two women in your life at the same table?' she said drily, following him out.

'I quail,' he admitted, but with a slight smile that was infinitely reassuring.

So much so that Kate decided to take the gamble: 'Or are there perhaps a few other women in your life that we should invite, to forestall any future confusion about who fits exactly where?'

'Well, there's always your mother,' he replied lightly. 'You could say she fits around the fringe of my life—by way of producing you.'

He and her mother had only met a few times when their paths had crossed socially, and to Kate's secret relief they had cordially disliked each other. Drake didn't like the way that her mother tried to dominate him with her relentless, battering logic, the way that she had hectored Kate as a child and still continued to denigrate her hopes and dreams as an adult, and Jane Crawford had hated that she couldn't influence his opinions or command his attention and respect and thus prove her superiority over the male sex. As a consequence she had been contemptuous of Drake's success, expressing cold disappointment that Kate should let her silly public infatuation for a 'chain-store novelist' destroy any hopes of her being taken seriously as a career woman.

But if Drake had been the kind of man to kowtow to her mother, Kate wouldn't have fallen in love with him.

'No, thanks.' She used the mocking offer as the springboard for her retaliation. 'But I am sorry that I'll never get the same chance of inviting the woman who produced *you* to dinner,' she said, just as lightly. 'That might have been interesting.'

His mouth twisted. 'No,' he said tightly, 'it wouldn't.'

'Of course not,' she sighed, half turning away to watch a dinghy being rowed out to one of the moored motor yachts.

'Because she only had one topic of conversation.'

'And what was that?' she asked carelessly, looking back at him, still expecting to be greeted by one of his usual witty evasions.

'Her husband. He was everything in the world to her, quite

literally. Even though he dumped her for another woman when I was six—walked out, divorced her, moved overseas to remarry and never contacted her again—she still clung to the fantasy that he was going to come back. She loved him therefore he must love her, and when the truth began to seep through the cracks of her obsession she blotted it out with drugs. She committed suicide when I was a teenager, not because she wanted to die, but because, according to the twisted reasoning in her note, she was proving to *him* how much she loved him, by showing that she couldn't live without him…'

It was a shock to hear the ugly story laid out so casually on a sunlit step. His almost clinical detachment made it sound as if he were discussing a plot in one of his books, but the underlying bleakness in his voice exposed it for the painful truth. No wonder he didn't like to talk about his childhood.

'I'm sorry,' Kate said, carefully reining in her sympathy. She looked out at the yacht, rocking now as the dinghy tied up alongside, fighting down her desire to pepper him with questions, trying to act as if his personal revelations were an everyday occurrence. 'I had no idea.'

'Few do…fortunately I'd legally changed my name as soon as I was old enough, so my past stops there. The press find PR rumours more interesting anyway; no one cares about tracing some kid called Richardson.' He shrugged, following her gaze to the activities of the oarsman in his bright orange life-jacket. 'You know what the real kicker was?' he murmured, after a moment.

She remained silent, afraid of stemming the dark tide of words.

'When her husband left her, my mother thought that she could use me to keep him tied to her for ever. But instead he simply cut his losses, and immediately had another son, to replace the one he'd left behind. While my mother was telling me to set a place for Daddy every night, he was creating a whole, shiny new family for himself in Australia—two boys and a girl. So when he finally found out his crazy ex-wife had killed herself he wasn't interested in being foisted with the product of her tainted love. And since there was no one else to claim me, I went into the foster-care system…'

'Her husband'… She noticed how he never said 'my father'—and Kate couldn't blame him. Since her parents had separated even before she was born she had not been a witness to any emotional carnage. At least she and her genial, happy-go-lucky father had had some contact with each other over the years—mostly letters exchanged behind her mother's disapproving back, and the occasional visit to the islands when she had been old enough to afford to pay, since Barry Crawford was chronically short of money and could rarely be bothered to bestir himself from beneath his beloved palm trees. Her father hadn't wanted the rights or responsibility of custodial parenthood, but he hadn't ignored her whole existence!

She darted a look at the chiselled perfection of Drake's profile, her heart aching for him, and for her baby. No longer did it surprise her that Drake had always been so bitterly opposed to having a family. In his experience love and marriage were associated with obsession and abandonment, with children merely pawns or weapons in their parents' hands.

He turned his head, capturing her sideways glance, and raised a quizzical eyebrow.

'Shall we say six o'clock for dinner?'

'Yes, all right,' she murmured, taken off guard by the sudden switch from the momentous to the mundane.

'We keep country hours here in Oyster Beach,' he said, and

strolled away while she was still grappling with her new perspective on his life.

Had that little bout of unaccustomed openness been a bribe or an enticement? she wondered as she watched him go. A warning or an invitation? Either way he must know he had her hooked.

She approached his house that evening with some trepidation, but, to her surprise, Kate enjoyed the dinner, and the company. After some slight initial stiltedness the atmosphere had relaxed as the conversation had inevitably turned to books and become wide-ranging and general. Drake looked askance at her when she refused a glass of wine, but he readily accepted the excuse of her illness earlier in the day, and when her offer to help Melissa in the kitchen was snapped up he seemed bemused.

'I didn't know you could cook,' he said as she expertly whisked up a sauce for the vegetables.

'You never asked.' He knew damned well that he had been careful to steer well clear of cosy, domestic settings. They had always dined out or at his hotel when they were together. 'Actually, I'm a superb cook.'

She was slightly smug when she saw that Melissa had taken the easy way and crumbed the scallops but the meal was delicious and her compliments sincere.

By the time she wended her way back home under a star-pricked sky she was well pleased with her performance. She had played it low-key with Drake and not made any attempt at intimacy, conspiring tacitly with Melissa to keep the conversation away from the personal and firmly focused on more entertaining issues.

After dinner, instead of sophisticated banter they had engaged in an argumentative game of Scrabble in which Kate had been ignominiously crushed by the two fiercely competitive professionals. However, a round of Trivial Pursuit had given her the chance to trounce them both and restored her buckled self-esteem.

The perfect ending to a slightly traumatic and wholly enlightening day.

CHAPTER SEVEN

THE next week was a curious mixture of good and bad. For two days after Melissa left Kate didn't see hide nor hair of Drake, but she did see a great deal of his hairy companion.

'What's the matter, Prince, is he ignoring you, too?' she asked on the third morning, putting down a plastic bowl with the meagre trimmings of the meat she had cooked the previous night, mixed with some boiled rice.

After finding the light rubbish bin outside the kitchen door tipped over and the scallops chewed out of their newspaper wrapping and left scattered on the grass, she had roundly scolded the dog, who had managed to look so downcast at being accused of the crime that she had relented and started feeding him more substantial snacks.

If Drake objected to her suborning his dog he could come over and complain about it but, as he had pointed out, Prince was a shameless scavenger and was probably fed by locals up and down the beach.

Since she had always lived in places with restrictions on owning animals Kate had never had a furred pet, but she was determined her child would have more than a goldfish to cuddle and love. Not an energy-sucking giant like Prince, but something suitable for a small yard. Trained to be

careful with money, Kate had saved up more than enough
for a deposit on an older do-up in one of the outer suburbs,
or a town house with a back garden in one of the newer in-
tensive-housing developments. She knew she couldn't
expect emotional or financial support from her mother, and
she still had no idea what to expect from Drake. Things
might be tough for a while if she had to go it alone, but she
would cope.

'You should tell your owner that all work and no play
makes Drake a very dull boy,' she suggested to Prince as he
wolfed down the food in two bites and overturned the bowl
to make sure he hadn't missed anything.

She wondered if she had made a mistake in thinking that
Drake's confidences of the other day might herald a promis-
ing new phase in their relationship.

'But dull is relative, I suppose,' she told the dog.

No doubt Drake was deeply engaged in some death-
defying heroics via his latest alter-ego. His thrillers weren't
written as a series linked by the same central characters, as
many other, highly successful thriller-writers chose to do.
Drake rebuilt his world from the ground up with every book.
Each featured a new cast, new country, new conflict…and a
new girlfriend to betray the hero, or to be kidnapped, tortured,
murdered or otherwise threatened in an attempt to subvert his
desperate cause. Innocence was no defence in Drake Daniels'
novels. It always seemed to presage disaster for the woman
when any of Drake's cynical heroes began developing tender
feelings towards her, and making plans for the future.

*The way he dumps his girlfriends in real life when they start
getting too close, and demanding too much of his attention,*
she mused.

'Perhaps I'm better off with him being wary and suspicious,' she said to Prince. 'Do you think I should just tell him about being pregnant and brazen it out, or lead up to it gradually and risk him accusing me of trying to trick him?'

Prince thought she should wear a plastic bowl on her head and roll around on the grass, and then dash down to the beach and dig holes.

Kate declined, but she did allow him to tag along when she went for her afternoon walk, and on the way back around the flat, rocky point she met Drake coming towards her.

'So this is where you are!' he declared, halting. He was wearing faded khaki hiking shorts and a Hawaiian shirt hanging open over his tanned chest, the sheen of perspiration on his skin indicating that he had been walking briskly.

'Are you talking to the dog, or to me?' said Kate, looking up at him from the shade of her straw hat. 'I thought you were busy working.'

'I've been working since six a.m. I'm taking a short break.' He picked up a stick of driftwood and threw it towards the sea. Prince sat and watched it arc over and hit the wet sand just in front of the waves, then trotted over and gummed it up, delivering it back to Drake with an air of patient long-suffering that made Kate snicker.

'I've never seen a dog be sarcastic before. I didn't ask him to come, you know, he just followed me,' she said, warmed by the thought that he had missed either of them.

Drake turned and fell in beside her as she picked her way through the scattered stones. 'You don't "ask" Prince to do anything, he'll do just what he damned well pleases—how do you think he got his name?'

She knew from the offhand warmth in his tone that 'Prince' was a term of affection, not derision.

'I thought it was because of his regal bearing,' she said, as

Prince 'wuffed' into a pile of rotting seaweed, his three legs scrabbling madly as he skated on the slimy mass.

Drake laughed. 'You wouldn't believe it now but he can actually look almost respectable when that coat has just been groomed. The problem is, it only lasts five minutes—until he can find the nearest pile of dirt.'

'That's because he doesn't want to be respectable, he wants to have fun.'

'Don't we all?' said Drake with a silky nuance, sliding his hand down his bare chest in a way that reminded her of that day in the car. Her temperature shot up and she failed to look where she was going.

'Careful!' Drake caught her elbow as her sneakered foot skidded into a rock pool.

'Oh!' Kate lifted her dripping foot and then looked into a pool. 'Oh, look—hermit crabs.' Her sundress fluttered around her knees as she crouched down for a closer look at the tiny creatures, humping their houses on their backs. 'They remind me of you,' she teased, testing one with her finger and watching him retreat back into the depths of the spiral shell.

'Clever, adaptive survivalists?'

'Hard-shelled and soft-centred.'

'You think I'm soft-centred?' He sounded as if he didn't know whether to be amused or appalled, his hand remaining on her elbow as he tugged her back to her feet to resume their walking.

'You must be, or you wouldn't need such a hard shell,' she teased. 'Well, semi-soft, anyway,' she amended to hide the shock as she realised the stunning truth of her words. As cynical and tough as he made himself out to be, at his core Drake felt himself vulnerable; that was why he erected so many defences.

'Actually, at the moment, I'd class myself as semi-hard,' he said, pointedly looking at the sway of her breasts against the low-cut dress.

'Drake!' She looked furtively around the beach, resisting the urge to place her hands across her chest like a Victorian maiden.

'Oh, look, cat's eyes!' He diverted her from her confusion, stooping to pick one of the convex shells up from a shallow pool, holding it for her to see the iridescent trapdoor at the bottom pulling into place, before gently putting it back in the water. 'It reminds me of you,' he mimicked her teasing tone.

She wrinkled her nose. 'Great, I'm like a sea-snail.'

'Beautiful and functional, what more can you ask?'

'I'm not beautiful,' she denied. 'Not like my mother.'

'No, thank God—she's like a perfect line drawing, sharp and flat, whereas you're like a watercolour—delicate and subtle, yet vibrant with colour and life, with deeper shades of meaning than appear at first glance.'

'You are quick with your similes this afternoon,' she said, trying to prick the dangerous bubble of joy that threatened her determinedly casual façade. 'Does that mean you're still working? I hope you brought your notebook with you.' She tilted her head back to see and laughed, because—sure enough—there was a tell-tale rectangle outlined in the back pocket of his shorts.

His fingers intertwined with hers, giving them a faint punishing squeeze.

'You don't like being compared to your mother, do you?'

'We're all a product of our parents; I suppose we can't avoid it,' said Kate, her voice softening as she thought of their baby. Was this the moment to broach the subject?

'But, as Shakespeare said, "comparisons are odorous"—'

'I thought they were odious.' Kate was pleased to have caught him out, still smarting from her drubbing at Scrabble.

'That was John Donne, not Shakespeare,' he topped her for smugness. 'He actually said: "She, and comparisons are odious", which sums up your mother even better!'

'For someone who's dyslexic, you sure read a lot,' she complained, unoffended. She remembered an interview where he'd said that, when working way out in the boonies, reading had been one of the few forms of safe entertainment, the only other options for a bunch of misfit males thrown together for the duration of a dirty job being drinking, gambling and fighting. He'd seen a few men die from their choice of amusement.

He grinned. 'I cheat. I have a book of quotations lying on my desk. Some of my heroes have fought some very erudite villains,' he informed her.

Kate laughed and he continued, after a slight pause, to say offhandedly: 'I never had any help with my dyslexia as a kid—we moved around too much, and after the drug-taking started my mother never bothered whether I was at school. But when I was older I found out for myself how to get around the barriers, and I read whatever and wherever I could.'

'Is your dyslexia inherited from your mother or your father?' she asked without thinking.

There was only a brief falter in his stride. 'I have no idea.'

'I'm sorry; I didn't mean to pry,' she said, feeling the mental shutters start to come down.

'I don't remember being read to as a child, if that means anything,' he said abruptly. 'But there were plenty of other explanations for that—my mother always scurrying around, frantically making sure we had everything *just so* for her husband, so that he wouldn't lose his temper when he got home, tired out from work and found that everything wasn't perfect—or, rather, he was tired out from his *mistress* as my mother found out on the day he left—' He came to a dead stop in the sand, stiffening, and Kate thought he was angry at having said more than he had meant to and was about to storm off, but then she saw he was watching Prince, who had rushed into the chilly sea to snap at the small rush of waves generated by the wake of a passing launch, and was now heading back towards them at a rolling clip.

'No, Prince—!' he ordered sternly, dropping her hand and stepping forward as the floppy ears started to rotate, but it was too late and the dog's whole body went into violent convulsions, the shaggy wool letting fly a hail of cold sea water mixed with gritty sand that made Kate shriek.

'Damn dog!' cursed Drake, mopping down his spattered chest with the corner of his shirt.

'He was only doing what comes naturally.' Prince's inherent instability had toppled him backwards into a heap on the sand and Kate started forward to help him up. 'Oh, you poor—'

Drake flung up a barring arm. 'Don't—you'll hurt his pride,' and they watched the dog roll over and bounce up as if falling over had been his intention all along.

Kate looked at him wryly. 'Don't tell me—it's a guy thing!' She brushed at the grainy wet spots on her dress and took off her hat to shake it out.

'You look as if you have freckles,' said Drake, running his thumb across her bare collar-bone, smearing a row of dots. He bent and put his mouth where his thumb had been, his tongue dipping into the sensitive crease between her collar-bone and slender throat. 'Mmm, you taste much saltier than usual.'

'What are you doing?' Kate shivered, pushing his head away, his dark hair silking against her palm.

'Trying to help you clean up,' he said innocently, his eyes

anything but innocent. 'Why don't you come up to the house and I'll dry you off properly?'

She had been so absorbed in their conversation she hadn't realised that they had walked all the way back.

'Thank you, but I have a perfectly adequate towel at my place,' she said, clutching her hat to her breasts.

The sultry look in his eyes kindled into wicked amusement. 'I wasn't thinking of using a towel.'

She gave him a haughty look. 'I know, and, as I said, I can look after myself. You need to get back to work and I—I—have things to do.' He had said he was taking a short break and she didn't want to give him any further excuse to accuse her of being disruptive to his writing routine. She knew from his own description of his methods that he worked in sustained bursts of intense concentration. It was important that he know *she* knew the difference between her presence being distracting and being destructive. Then he might even start to see that she could be a positive, supportive element in his working life…

'What things?' Strong legs planted in the sand, arms akimbo, bright shirt flaring around his gorgeous bare torso, he was an almost irresistible temptation. She firmly beat it down. For all she knew, this seductive teasing might merely be a test on his part, to see how much of his attention she intended to demand.

'Just…things. *Female* things,' she added cunningly—words to make most men blanch and run.

He didn't budge, his eyes on her hands, nervously scrunching her hat. 'Are you *afraid* of me, Kate?' he murmured, half curious, half taunting.

She decided on the truth. 'Yes,' she said, shaking her hair back behind her ears and replacing her slightly crumpled hat, like a warrior putting on a defensive helmet. 'I don't *know* you—'

He was *en garde* even before she had fully unsheathed her words. 'You know me well enough to make love to,' he pointed out.

'I—it's different here...*you're* different,' she said, trying to marshal all the things she wanted to say in the right order.

'I thought you said you wanted something "different",' he said sarcastically. 'Have you changed your mind again?'

'Yes, I mean no—'

His patience snapped. 'Well, when you *do* decide to make up your mind, let me know!'

This time he did stump off, and she thought he might disappear into himself again for another few days, but to her surprise and subdued delight, the next afternoon when she went walking at roughly the same time he appeared again, and the next...each time a little earlier in her walk until by the end of the week they were setting off together.

Walking and talking was certainly much more productive than sitting and talking, the relaxed surroundings and lack of watchful eyes making Kate realise how proscribed their lives had become in the city.

Most of their talk was idle and unthreatening, but inevitably they touched on weightier subjects and Kate began to amass more pieces of the puzzle that made up Drake Daniels. Like the fact that when he had shed the name of Richardson he had also sloughed off his Christian name, Michael, and had deliberately chosen a name that had no connection with either his father or his mother—one that was sufficiently different to satisfy his hunger to be unique, to be more than the nobody his parents had reduced him to by their destructive indifference.

Drake had been a defiantly swashbuckling name to his younger self, he admitted wryly, and Daniels had been the name of the only adult whom he had respected, a high-school English teacher who had seen a special spark in the troubled youth that no one else had bothered to nurture, and whom he had attempted to encourage, challenge and inspire in the short time that they had shared a classroom, advising him to travel as far and widely as he could to expand his human experience for his future writings.

They occasionally met other people on their strolls, who either casually greeted Drake by name or failed to recognise him at all, and Kate learned that the ebb and flow of tourists at Oyster Beach dictated his puzzling annual schedule—summers for travel and research and roughly drafting out ideas, the rest of the year fitting in periods of intensive writing at Oyster Beach in a way that avoided both school and public holiday breaks.

One afternoon at low tide, after they had walked in the other direction to the mouth of the tidal estuary, they came across three shrieking little boys digging trenches in the wet sand near the waterline.

'They don't look old enough to be out here on their own,' said Kate, estimating them to be no more than five, one of them a toddler still in nappies. She glanced up at Drake, who was staring broodingly at the sandy trio. 'And don't tell me things are done differently here in the country.'

'I wasn't going to.' He was scanning the straggle of houses tucked into the trees behind the low dunes and then out to sea. 'Ah…' He pointed to a lone female figure lying up in the dunes, nestled into a hollow by a log, protecting the pages of her book against the ruffle of the light breeze.

'I hope she's paying more attention to the children than she is to her book,' worried Kate. 'Young children can drown very quickly in only a few centimetres of water.'

She went over to talk to the trio about their endeavours and felt better when she saw the woman instantly put her book aside and sit up, responding to a reassuring wave by relaxing back on her elbows, but not resuming her reading until Kate moved away, hurrying to join the man who had dawdled on ahead.

'Can't be one of my books—or she wouldn't have been able to put it down so easily,' jibed Drake as Kate fell into step beside him.

'Why didn't you come down and say hello? They would have liked a man to admire their work.'

'No, thanks. I told you, kids aren't my thing. Why do you think I always come back to town during school holidays?'

'I thought it was to avoid all their parents. It's not as if the little ones know or care that you're the great Drake Daniels. They're completely unpretentious. That toddler was so cute the way he tried to copy his brothers—'

'A total pain in the neck, if you ask me,' he said tersely.

'How can you say that?'

'Drop it, Kate,' he ordered, but then he was the one unable to leave it alone. 'Since when were you so keen on ankle-biters, anyway? I thought you agreed with me that they don't fit in with a career-orientated lifestyle.'

'But lifestyles don't always stay the same throughout people's lives,' she argued. 'They're constantly being modified by changing circumstances, like having children...'

'If people *want* to change. Some people should never have children,' he said flatly. 'Especially when they don't have the time or inclination to care for them, or because social pressures and vanity or self-interest—or simply pure careless-ness—come into play.'

Kate's heart staggered. 'At that rate neither of us would have been born,' she said, desperately trying to put a positive spin on his words, 'and think what the world would have missed...'

He didn't respond to the opportunity to use his usual amusing wit. 'And think of all those parents who buy into the perfect baby fantasy and then find the day-to-day reality turns them into abusive monsters!' he grated. 'Call me a heartless bastard, but I don't ever want to add any kids to the list of my mistakes.'

No, not heartless—but maybe one who cared too much, thought Kate shakily. In spite of what he said, she didn't believe it was solely a matter of preserving his highly enjoyable lifestyle. Drake seemed convinced that he would not be a good parent. He was an intelligent man—he must know that he wasn't doomed to perpetuating his parents' weaknesses and failures, yet it appeared that he wasn't prepared to put himself to the touch.

Kate had far more trust in him than he did in himself. She knew that, whatever happened, he would never punish an innocent child for an adult's mistakes. Although cynicism ran strongly through his books, they were essentially heroic stories of men who found personal redemption in a worthy cause. She only hoped that Drake would find it worth redeeming himself for the sake of his own child.

She could have let herself be depressed by his vow to eternally shun fatherhood, but by the end of the stroll her natural resilience had reasserted itself, boosted by Drake's relentless flirting. Because she had fallen eagerly into bed with him the first time they had met, she realised that she had missed out on the seductive excitement that she was now experiencing as with a look, a word or a touch Drake attempted to evoke reminders of the powerful physical attraction that existed between them. She had deprived herself of the delicious torment of the should she/shouldn't she nervousness and the romantic thrill of the chase the first time around, so why shouldn't she enjoy it to the full in the precious little time she had left?

Her only previous serious relationship had been with a newly qualified lawyer who had sought her out at a party just after her nineteenth birthday, and laid gentle siege to her reserve. Brett had been flatteringly devoted for long enough to make her start to wonder if they might get engaged, but when she had finally been persuaded to reluctantly introduce him to her mother he had been off like a shot, resurfacing a few weeks later as one of Jane Crawford's new crop of hotshot legal protégés.

At the time she had thought Brett the height of romance, but he had never made her bones melt and her flesh quicken, as Drake could do with a single, smouldering look.

It was slightly disconcerting to discover in herself a streak of cruelty that took pleasure in his frustration as she continued to keep him at arm's length.

When he offhandedly suggested on their Friday walk that Kate might like to come to the planned pool game that evening after all, he clearly expected her to be instantly charmed by the idea.

'Will the others be bringing women, too?'

'Not that I know of—what's that got to do with it?'

She lowered her eyelashes demurely. 'Well, I wouldn't want to start a fight.'

He snorted.

'I thought I was supposed to stay away from Steve Marlow in case he dragged me into a life of degradation and crime.'

'Maybe I over-stated the case a bit,' he admitted.

'Are you going to win?'

His diffidence disappeared. 'Of course! They're rank

amateurs—they just like to think they're hustlers!' he said, oozing male hubris.

'And you want me along to provide the applause for your victory?' she teased, touched by the notion that he wanted her to see him as the conquering hero. Or maybe he just wanted to prove to them both that he wasn't jealous. 'Do I get to pin my favour to your sleeve?'

'Not unless you want me to get beaten up. It's a pub not a jousting ring.'

'Will I be able to play…since you told Steve Marlow that I couldn't? Or will I have to stand around holding your beer?'

'*Can* you play?' he asked, looking so surprised she was tempted to lie simply for the pleasure of seeing his face.

'No, but I can learn.'

He looked vaguely hunted. Obviously his impulsive invitation was becoming more complicated than he had planned.

'Or if you think you might need help, I could just wear something short and low-cut and lean on the table whenever the others line up their shots,' she offered sweetly.

His eyes creased as he imagined the graceful Kate Crawford vamping it up as the local pub tart. 'Or you could just wear nothing at all and we'll forget about going to play pool,' he murmured with a wicked grin.

He grinned again when he saw the prim white shirt and blue trousers she put on to go to the pub, her white sandals showing off small feet with innocently unpainted toenails. 'That's my girl,' he chuckled.

Am I? Kate wanted to say. *Am I really?*

It was a rowdy night unlike any she had ever spent and she really enjoyed it once she had stopped being polite and simply shouted like everyone else, to be heard over the local band rocking the rafters and the bawling exchanges, catcalls and shouts of laughter. There were lots of jeans and flip-flops and more men than women, but the atmosphere was buzzing and Kate quickly discovered that a locally made, no-alcohol spiced beer was the choice of brew for designated drivers and wowsers alike, for very good reason.

She was on her second delicious glass when Ken and Steve arrived—minus partners but hugely amused to see Kate tucked up to Drake's side—and they all listened to a few songs from the band while waiting for the pool table they had booked to become free. Although there were a few grins and knowing hails from the crowd, mostly aimed at Steve, it was all very laid-back, and there were no intrusive approaches or fuss about the fame in their midst. Everyone was just there to enjoy themselves at full volume. It was a little quieter in the back room of the pub where the pool tables were, but that changed when Steve kept feeding coins into the jukebox in the corner, ordering Kate to pick the songs most guaranteed to annoy Drake. So she chose dreamy, romantic ballads punctuated with the occasional head-banger to appease the good-natured groans from around the room.

In spite of Drake's earlier boasts, his two friends made him work for his wins—mainly because they kept ganging up to ruin his concentration when he was playing one or other of them. Remembering her comments about leaning on the table, Kate enjoyed looking at the provocative pull of Drake's faded jeans as they stretched across his tautly muscled backside when he bent to use his cue, and when he had a difficult shot facing her she made sure he knew she was staring down the open neck of his shirt, her own fingers playing suggestively in the V of her collar. However, he got his own back when chalking the tip of his cue, and she hurriedly primmed her mouth and pretended not to understand his sensual stroking and the deliberation with which he held her eyes while he gently blew off the excess chalk.

In the interests of fair play, Kate declared herself strictly neutral in the cheerfully insulting male byplay over the game and ferried cardboard tubs of hot chips and battered fish, jugs of beer and bottles of soft drinks to the protagonists, fascinated by the easy camaraderie between the three men, despite the fact that, as Steve pointed out, they were rarely all in the area at the same time. She enjoyed watching the differences in their play and chatting with each as they sat out games, but finally the series came down to a single match between Steve and Drake, while Ken kept up a hushed commentary that had Kate in fits of laughter.

Her sides were still aching when they drove back through the black, shadowy hills to the beach. Drake turned on the CD player and Kate was content to lie back and dream impossible dreams to the caress of some moody blues and the humming vibration of the Land Rover's engine.

Wrapped in a sensuous cloud of happy imaginings she was almost dozing when Drake murmured that they were home, and insisted on walking with her to her door.

'Enjoy yourself?'

'You know I did. I like your friends.'

'I noticed,' he said, but without any heat. 'They liked you, too.'

She sighed with a strange contentment. 'Steve said the three of you don't get together very often any more,' she said, unlocking the front door. A lot of Oyster Beach people didn't bother to lock their doors, at least in the off-season, she had been told, but Kate's cautionary habits were too deeply ingrained.

'No, but when we do it's always as if we only saw each other yesterday. The group dynamics are such we can just pick up where we left off. Some friendships are like that.'

'That's what we do, too, isn't it? Pick up where we left off,' she said, turning in the doorway. But not any more, she thought wistfully.

'Aren't you going to ask me in?' he suggested softly as she switched on the light and blinked at him like an owl, her silver eyes still hazed with dreams. 'Offer me a nightcap?'

'I don't have any alcohol in the house,' she said, hypnotised by his slow smile.

'A coffee, then.' He reached out and stroked her hair behind her ear, his thumb briefly brushing the lobe. 'Isn't that the way the two of us usually end a night out?'

No. They usually ended it in bed, making love. Her eyes dilated with betraying speed, her pink lips parting, her breasts rising and falling against the white cotton shirt.

'Coffee keeps me awake,' she croaked.

'That's good. Awake is good,' he murmured, slowly lowering his head, his thighs bumping against hers as he shuffled her back against the wooden panels of the open door. 'I wouldn't like you to be asleep when I did this…'

His kiss was warm, soft, sweet and sensuous…a delicate tasting of her resistance, with no aggression to trigger her alarm, just a gentle teasing of her lips, a whisper-soft stroke of his firm, velvety mouth.

It was so sweet and so soft it left her wanting, and as he began to draw back her arms slid around his waist and folded across his strong back, holding him secure while she went on tiptoe to try and increase the pressure against her yearning mouth.

He didn't make the mistake of swooping inside with his tongue, instead he withheld himself, luring her to seek her own pleasure and move ever deeper into danger.

His legs shifted, his knee bending as his denim thigh eased between hers, rising up to fit snugly into the notch of her body, his hands on her hips tilting her pelvis into the cradle of his and then stroking around to trace the outline of her panties through the thin fabric of her silk trousers. When he began to softly knead the rounded cheeks of her bottom, moving her rhythmically against the rigid muscles of his thigh, she uttered a tiny, shivery cry that broke on the still night.

'Ask me inside…take me to your bed,' he whispered, sipping the cry from her bee-stung lips. A clever glide of his fingers slipped a few of the pearl buttons on her shirt and she felt the delicate swirl of his fingertips on the silky swell of her tightening breast. 'You know you want to, Kate. You won't even have to ask, you just have to want me…I'm yours for the taking…all of me is yours…' He moved his hips in a slow rotation that rubbed the thick bulge between his legs against her feminine mound, teasing her with the memory of the turbulent ecstasy his heat and hardness could provide.

For a moment they both thought the faint squeak was her whimper of surrender, but then Kate groaned and turned her cheek to the door, her arms dropping away. She could feel Drake's rigid body drawn so tight it was trembling, then he uttered a harsh sound and let his forehead rap on the door behind her averted head, leaning it there while he said thickly:

'I can't take much more of this. I thought we were lovers, Kate. What's happening? Why can't we make love?' He lifted his head, temper seeking a safer outlet. 'And what the hell is that infernal noise?'

Now the enchanted spell was well and truly broken. 'A rat, I think,' she said. 'I told you about it, remember.'

'You've told me so many things…except, apparently, the one thing that really matters.' He pushed himself away from the door, breathing deeply, half turning away to hide the painful state of his body. 'Just tell me this, at least: have you fallen in love with someone else, Kate? Someone who makes it impossible for you to be with me?'

'No!' She fumbled with the buttons on her blouse. 'I— No— There's only ever been you these past two years. Please, just give me a little more time,' she begged.

'You haven't been raped, have you?' he rasped.

'What? *No!*' she said, her eyes rounded in shock. 'You're letting your imagination run away with you.'

'That's what I'm paid for,' he growled. 'You still want what we have, Kate. Stop fighting it. Whatever it is that's bugging you you'd better sort it out soon. Or I will.

'And first thing tomorrow I'm going to sort out that damned rat of yours!'

CHAPTER EIGHT

WHEN Kate walked into the house the next afternoon her heart jumped to find Drake standing barefoot in the middle of her kitchen, looking rumpled and gorgeously surly in the same shirt and jeans he had worn the previous night.

'I thought I locked up when I left; how did you get in?' she said breathlessly, setting down the cardboard box and large plastic bag she was carrying by the leg of the table.

'The rental agent gave me a spare key for emergencies,' he admitted, eyeing her grumpily.

'You mean you could have come in here any time you wanted?' she said faintly, thinking of *1000 Tips For A Healthy Pregnancy,* which she thought she might have left open in the bathroom.

'I could but I haven't— *I* respect people's personal privacy,' he said pointedly, as if reading her mind. 'I haven't been pawing through your secrets. But I told you I'd be over to help you with your pest problem, and when you didn't answer your door I thought something might be wrong…'

'What—like something out of *Curse Of The Rat People*? Did you think I might be lying chewed up on the floor?' she said sceptically, hugging herself with the knowledge that he worried about her in her absence. So it wasn't entirely a case of 'out of sight, out of mind'…

'Besides, you said you'd be here *first thing*. It's now after lunch.' She toned down her sarcasm as she took in his slightly bloodshot eyes, and dissipated expression. 'Are you all right? You don't look so great.' Which was a lie—Drake always looked terrific, whatever his physical state. And she had never known him to be ill. He either had the constitution of an ox or, more likely, he downplayed and concealed his illnesses the way he did the rest of his vulnerabilities.

He ran a hand through his hair and scratched his grainy chin. 'I was up all night writing.' He glared at her with a mixture of accusation and bewilderment. 'I didn't crash out until six a.m. I've only just woken up.'

Oh, oo maybe she *had* been out of sight and mind for a while…

'That's not my fault,' she defended herself from his look. 'I didn't order you to go home and write yourself into a coma.'

'No, you just wound me up, pumped me full of adrenalin and kicked me loose. What else did you expect me to do?'

She looked quickly away, smoothing back her hair and composing her face into a cool expression. Not quickly enough, however, for he suddenly chuckled knowingly.

'Why, Kate, is that what *you* did last night? Go to bed and dream a little wet dream of me?' he taunted. 'What a waste, when the real thing was right there for the asking.'

'But then you wouldn't have got all those pages written,' she told him stoutly, fighting to keep the heat that suffused her body out of her face.

'Maybe I wouldn't have minded the sacrifice,' he said silkily.

'Well, *I* would—I don't want you to *sacrifice* anything for me,' she said with haughty pride. 'People who feel forced to surrender something they value for the sake of someone else generally tend to get bitter and twisted if things don't work out the way they planned. My mother says she sacrificed her valuable time and money to give me a good education, which I've wasted, and she never lets me forget it. So, no, thanks, don't make any grand gestures on my behalf...'

'Wow, I did hit a sore point, didn't I?' he murmured. 'I was only kidding. Once I'm in the grip of writing fever I just have to keep going until it runs its course. It's a very anti-social tendency so it's actually quite useful when inspiration strikes in the middle of the night.'

'I saw a light on up in your office when I got up for a glass of water some time around three,' she confessed, revealing her own somewhat restless night. 'I thought you had probably just forgotten to turn it off.'

He had shown her his office the night of their scallop dinner—a large, book-lined, high-ceilinged room upstairs in the back corner of the house, with folding doors that opened onto a balcony shared with his bedroom, facing directly out to the beach. There was also a window on the other external wall, which overlooked Kate's holiday haven and the north-eastern end of the beach, but it was fitted with reflector glass and motorised tilting shutters, which he usually kept closed. He didn't like to feel claustrophobically shut in when he was working, he said, but he needed the security of walls and at least the illusion of total privacy.

'It's probably still on now. When I get in the zone I don't even think about practicalities like light, heat, food, sleep. I work and drop. It can make me a bit of a bastard the next day, though.'

Crudely, but aptly put. 'Is that an apology?'

'No, an explanation. Which is more than you've given me.' He left her to digest the wider implications of his comment as his eyes fell to the carry-box by her feet, which had begun to shudder and squeak.

'What in the—?' His eyes shot back to her face. 'You caught the rat yourself!' His surprise had a tiny suggestion of chagrin—St George deprived of his dragon.

She smiled wryly. 'Sort of.' She bent down to unfold the handles and reef open the top.

'You're not going to let it go after all that—?' Drake lapsed into silence as he noticed the Vet Clinic's stamp on the flap of the box in the same moment that a ball of furiously squeaking fur bounced out onto the faded floor and resolved itself into a small, glossy black kitten with a white breast and underbelly, and four white paws that immediately scampered into motion.

'A kitten? You went and got *that* little thing from Ken to catch a rat?' said Drake incredulously as he watched the creature skitter around a table leg. 'I hate to tell you this, sweetheart, but you've been suckered—it'll be eaten alive.' The kitten turned in response to the deep rumble of his voice, approaching his bare feet with the little black tail held high, wagging eagerly back and forth, and the squeaking redoubling in volume.

'That *is* my rat,' Kate told him with a rueful look at her night-time nemesis. 'I didn't get it *from* Ken; I took it *to* him.'

It had been a very uncomfortable trip, too, with the kitten squeaking in protest at being cooped up in the semi-dark again, poking a pathetic white paw through the tiny ventilating gap she had created in one of her suitcases by loosely tying the two zip fasteners together.

She watched the black tail start to wag even faster as Drake scooped up the kitten in one big hand, and cupped it level with his face, inspecting the small, triangular face with the yellow eyes and tiny white moustache angled crookedly under a black nose.

'When I opened the door under the house to shine the torch in, she came rushing out, squeaking to beat the band. Ken said she's not as young as she looks—several months at least—but she must have been hiding under the house and coming out at night scavenging for food, and then got trapped under there somehow in the last few days. He says she's lost a little bit of body weight, so he's given me some supplements to add to her food.' She nudged the plastic bag with her sneakered foot.

The kitten suddenly lunged forward and began swiping her piquant little face back and forth against Drake's nose, nuzzling his mouth in between squeaks.

'I think she likes you.' Kate laughed as Drake emerged from the flurry of friendliness spitting strands of black fur and hastily set the kitten back down on the floor to resume her exploration of the kitchen.

'Why can't she miaow like other cats?' he mumbled critically, still picking fur off his tongue. 'You'd have rescued her much sooner if she'd had the decency to behave like a proper feline.'

'I don't know, but I think it's cute,' she said defensively. 'Ken says not all cats vocalise in the same way—he said it could be physiological, or because she hasn't been around other cats who miaow. He said she must have been in good condition when she got trapped under the house or she wouldn't still have fat stores left in her body, so she's either a very good hunter or someone's pet, but no one had been asking about missing kittens.' She smiled as the animal made a daring pounce on a patch of sunlight.

'Ken seems to have said an awful lot,' he remarked, eyes narrowing on her softened face as he crossed his arms across his chest. Her gaze jumped to his. 'So how come *you* still have the cat and not him?' he pressed. 'Didn't you take it to the clinic to hand it in?'

Kate's gaze slid away from his and she busied herself un-packing the plastic bag. 'Well, yes…but Ken gave Koshka a thorough check-over and all the tests, and there's nothing actually wrong with her—the nurse gave her a good brushing and she doesn't even have fleas!' She darted him a triumphant look that was met with lowered brows.

'Koshka? You've given her a name already?'

'It's Russian for cat. Ken was calling her Kitty—I had to give her something prettier than that!' she insisted.

'Oh, yes, he knows all the right triggers.' His voice dripped with sarcasm as he shook his head. 'Don't tell me he persuaded you to adopt it?' he growled. 'What's going to happen when you go home? You're not allowed pets in your town house.'

'I know that. I'm not keeping her—just fostering for a few weeks, until I leave, or Ken can find her a home…'

Drake rolled his eyes. 'Where have I heard *that* one before?'

'He said she'd be kept alone in a cage if she stayed at the clinic, whereas here she can prowl and play, and we'll be good company for each other,' she hastened to add.

'You already have company—me. Not to mention my faithful hound.' His mouth took on a malicious curl. 'I guess the problem will be solved soon enough. Koshka won't be more than a single gulp for Prince.'

Kate gasped, and even though she knew he was joking she protectively snatched up her little charge, cuddling the warm, squirming body into the curve of her neck, laughing softly when a raspy tongue began to lap at the side of her jaw. She didn't notice the bloodshot brown eyes darken with a moody bleakness as Drake watched the tender byplay.

'We won't let that big goof get you, will we, Koshka?' she crooned, tickling a white chin and letting small, sharp teeth gnaw at her scratching finger, the wagging tail beating a light tattoo against her breast. 'Mummy will look after you.'

'Foster-mummy,' corrected Drake. 'You'll get attached— how are you going to feel when you have to give her back?'

'I'll cross that bridge when I come to it,' said Kate, letting the cat scamper free to investigate the hall, jogged by his abrupt tone into remembering that he, too, had been fostered. She hoped that after the horror of his mother's suicide, he had passed into loving hands, but the indications were unfortunately otherwise. He obviously had no trust in maternal figures.

'What do you know about caring for a cat?'

'Not much, but I bought a book at the clinic, and I'm sure it's largely a matter of practical common sense. I have plenty of that,' she reminded him.

'She'll shed all over your clothes. You'll hate that. You're very fastidious.'

'I'm not compulsive about it, and cats are fastidious creatures, too—they're always cleaning themselves. Anyway, who cares about a bit of stray fluff when they're on holiday?'

'It'll get on the furniture, too. The landlord might object.'

'She's a short-hair so it shouldn't be too much of a problem, but I did buy one of those sticky rollers from Ken's receptionist just in case,' she admitted.

'Boy, they really saw you coming, didn't they? How many cat toys did you buy?' he said, moving over to peer into the top of the bag.

'A few,' she said, batting away his hands and scrunching it closed to hide the embarrassing profusion of balls, catnip treats and clockwork mice. She gave him a very cool look. 'They're educational.'

'She's a cat; you're not going to turn her into Einstein

in a few weeks. She might wag her tail like a dog, but the similarity ends there. You can't train cats the way you can train dogs.'

'You mean *some* dogs. Your dog doesn't seem to be very well trained.'

'Oh, so we're reduced to insulting each other's pets now, are we? Prince is a supreme individualist—he knows what he's supposed to do, he just doesn't want to do it.'

'Like master, like pet,' she told him cattily.

'So, I guess that makes you cute and soft and cuddly, then,' he said, with an insinuating smile. She tossed her head at him and he laughed, banishing the last of the brooding shadows that had hung around him. 'You bristle just like a cat, too. I always thought of you as a cool, sinuous, haughty Siamese and now I'm finding out that you're a cosy little bundle of mixed-breed mischief. You even squeak when you're excited. You know, that little sound you make when you—'

'Oh, go write a novel, why don't you?' Kate said, shoving him towards the door. She had never blushed so much in her life as she had this last week. It had to be the over-excited hormones running riot in her bloodstream, upsetting her normal levels of biological self-containment.

'Thanks, I think I will.' He grinned, his eyes briefly shifting to focus on something in the middle distance, in a familiar sign of mental abstraction.

But just as she was resigned to having been eclipsed by his soaring imagination his gaze focused back on Kate's flustered face, and he hooked her around the waist, arching her lissom body back over his arm for a long, lush, lascivious kiss. He hadn't shaved or showered—he must have staggered straight out of the house from his bed—but Kate loved the sexy scrape of his jaw and the earthy male ripeness exuded by his hard body beneath the rumpled clothes. It made her think of long, sweaty nights of passionate exuberance and torrid delights.

'You said you haven't been with anyone but me since we met,' he murmured, his warm breath feeding into her mouth as he reminded her of the words she had blurted out last night. 'Was that true?'

'Of course it's true,' she sighed, knowing that to deny it now would be a gross self-betrayal. If the truth of her fidelity made him gloat it would at least show him capable at some level of enjoying normal human possessiveness without confusing it with pathological obsession. And if it made him feel nervous or trapped by the implied commitment on her part, then he would just have to deal with it!

'Quite a pair, aren't we?' She felt his smile shape her lips. 'Free to do what we please—and what we do is please each other so well that celibacy becomes an active pleasure when we're apart.' He broke away from her mouth and saluted her stunned brow with a departing kiss. 'I didn't stop looking at other women the night we met, but I certainly stopped wanting them—it's surprising how sexy a stretch of celibacy can be when you know what's waiting for you at the other end, or should I say *who*…?'

Having made his stupendous admission with breath-taking nonchalance, he cruised out the door, careful to close it against escaping felines.

Kate felt winded—and perversely betrayed. Her proud portrayal of serene indifference to all the gossip and rumours about other women had been a wasted effort. Drake *had* been faithful to their relationship despite the no-strings caveat he himself had insisted upon. For months…*years*…she had forced herself to accept his tacit policy of 'don't ask, don't tell' *when there had been nothing for Drake to tell*!

It was typical of Drake to slip her a life-altering revelation about himself under the guise of flippancy, and even more typical of him to disappear afterwards. The characters in his books might be dissected to within an inch of their lives, but in reality Drake preferred his own character armour to remain firmly in place and to dole out psychological insights with miserly reluctance. He knew that knowledge was power and he was very careful not to put the balance of power in any hands but his own. He had just handed a little more over to Kate. He would now pull up the drawbridge until he felt comfortable with what he had done.

She wasn't in the least surprised when she didn't see him for another day, and when he did reappear he made no reference to their previous conversation, dropping back into the safe realm of daily walks, teasing arguments and sexy banter and the occasional shared meal. There was a new physical awareness between them, however, unrelated to sexual tension that was always there in the background, and Kate knew that the next step was hers to take. She was in no hurry to make it, knowing that it could destroy the painstaking trust that they had been slowly building up, and take him away from her for ever. From attempting to seduce her at every turn, Drake was now playing a waiting game and she was slightly chagrined to recognise that she had half wanted him to take the decision out of her hands and use his sexual dominance to *force* her to tell him what he needed to know.

Drake continued to also hold himself aloof from Koshka's eager pursuit of his affections and after a few days of keeping the cat indoors, on Ken's advice, Kate was amused to see Prince as disdainful as his master of this pretender to the throne of her attention.

Koshka, however, wasn't in the least oppressed by her

failure to charm, the disparity in their sizes, or the supposed natural enmity between cats and dogs. Tail wagging, she would greet Prince with friendly squeaks whenever he appeared, trotting curiously in his shadow and ignoring his gummy show of yellow teeth when she tried to steal the scraps that fell from his food bowl. When he snored in his favourite shady spot beneath the hedge she would prowl over, batting at a floppy ear or sleepy twitch of the tail, and when he grandly ignored her teasing she would curl up beside him in a sunny spot of grass for a quick catnap before wandering off to find some fresh, feline challenge.

It was Koshka's habit of making sudden, thundering sprints up and down the house for no apparent reason that was the reason for Kate's literal, and figurative, downfall a few days later.

She was carrying her sun-lounger, book and water bottle down the verandah steps when a glossy black ball of lightning shot out of the house behind her and streaked between her feet, tripping her up and pitching her head first down the stairs. Her flailing hand made a frantic grab for the wooden hand-rail, but only her fingernails made painful contact with the splintered paint, throwing her at an angle over the side of the steps. Seeing the rocky garden edge looming up she desperately tried to twist and protectively curl up her body, missing the rocks but landing heavily on top of the metal bar of the sun-lounger, which had hit the ground sideways, unfolding as it fell.

She lay, dazed and breathless in a tangle of bent metal and canvas, the bar that had painfully folded her in two still jammed into her bare abdomen. It took her several attempts to struggle free but she eventually managed to roll over onto her back, weakly pushing away the wreckage of the lounger, wincing at the long scrapes she could feel on her hip, elbow and thigh. Her bikini top had been dislodged and she twisted it back into place, tiny beads of perspiration jumping out on her forehead as she became aware of an ominous, cramping pain low in her belly.

Koshka returned to nuzzle at the shiny pool of hair flared out around her head, and discover the delicious, salty moisture at her temples, and Kate raised her head to escape the gentle rasp of her abrasive tongue, bracing herself on one arm to start pushing herself upright.

Then a big hand was there, cupping her neck, a strong arm supporting her shoulders.

'My God, Kate—that bloody cat! I had the shutters open— I saw the whole thing. You could have broken your neck!' Drake knelt down beside her, shooing Koshka away as he helped her sit up, curving her against his supporting chest, brushing the dirt and grass clippings from her damaged side, anxiously tilting up her white face and examining her dazed eyes beneath the damp fringe sticking to her forehead, looking rather grey-faced himself. 'Just sit here for a moment; don't try to get up until you feel a bit steadier,' he said huskily. 'A knock like that can really take it out of you. Thank God you fell on that lounger and not on your head. Anything broken, you think?'

'No…' It was as much an answer as a thread of protest as he gently unfolded the arm that Kate had tucked protectively across her middle.

'Shall I carry you inside?'

'No, I want to stand up…I need to stand up,' she insisted shakily, hoping against hope that when she stretched out she would find that she was just experiencing a muscular spasm from the shock of the fall.

Murmuring reassurances, Drake helped her to her feet,

letting her lean on him as she tested her ankles and gingerly flexed her shoulders and wrists. To her relief the pulling pain in her stomach started to fade away, just as she'd hoped it would, once the blood started pumping freely around her extremities again.

They took it very slowly going back up the stairs, and when she limped back inside the house Drake made her lie down on the couch for a few minutes with her feet propped on a cushion. She accepted an offer of sweet tea when the alternative seemed to be having him hover over her or pace up and down. When Koshka wandered back inside innocent of all the commotion she had caused, Kate petted her forgivingly as she sipped her tea, covering the little ears to block out Drake's dark threats of discipline.

When she felt a little less fragile, she persuaded him to let her go and pull on a tee shirt over her bikini, but when she emerged from her bedroom she was white-faced again, fully dressed, wearing shoes, and carrying her purse.

'I think you'd better take me to the doctor,' she said thinly to Drake, who was standing in the kitchen stirring sugar into a mug of tea for himself.

'Why? What's the matter?' He put the mug down abruptly and strode over. Before he reached her side she went even paler, biting her lip and blinking hard as she dropped her purse and pressed both hands to her stomach.

'Oh, God—' she choked.

'What is it?' He slid his hands over the top of hers, feeling their icy tremor, fearing she was sliding into delayed shock. 'Come on, Kate, tell me,' he ordered harshly, to jolt her consciousness. 'Don't fade out on me—do you think you've hurt something inside?'

'Yes.' She looked at him, her silver eyes wild and tormented. 'The baby…I think something's happening to the baby!' She caught her breath on a frightened sob. 'I feel this pain in my side and all around my middle, like a tearing…I think I must have hurt my baby when I fell. Oh, God, what if I'm losing it? I don't want to lose my baby—'

'Baby? You're *pregnant*?' He looked as if he had been hit in the face, but his stunned bewilderment only lasted a split second and then he was as white-lipped as she, his eyes burning black holes in the stony mask of his face as he made all the right connections. 'You're carrying a child? *My* child? *That's* why you came to Oyster Beach?' He read the truth in her agonised expression. 'You want to have the baby and keep it? *Damn you all to hell, Kate!*' he exploded. He spun, slamming his fist against the wall.

She put her hand on the sleeve of his polo shirt, feeling the iron muscle underneath quivering with tension as his fist continued to grind against the caved wallboard. 'Please, can we talk about it later?' she begged his averted profile. 'I need to go to a doctor now and I suppose the nearest medical practice is in Whitianga—I don't think it's safe for me to drive. Drake?'

He didn't move and her fingers curled into the unyielding muscle. 'Unless you *want* your baby to die!' she cried in panicked desperation, shaking at his rigid arm. 'Maybe you're thinking that if you delay long enough you can force me into a miscarriage—get rid of the baby and save yourself some grief!'

He tore himself from her grasp and away from the wall, his handsome features for once ugly. 'If you believe I'm capable of murdering an innocent child for selfish gain, then what in the hell made you think I'd ever be any kind of fit father?' he said savagely. 'No, don't bother to answer that— you were going to sucker me into playing Daddy to your kid

and now you know better than to even try,' he added with incandescent fury. 'Where are your keys? We'll take your car—
it'll be quicker.'

He stopped, not looking at her as he demanded harshly;
'Are you bleeding?'

'No,' she said, breathing shallowly, 'but I have these sharp,
low-down, stabbing pains…'

This time there was no supportive arm around her shoulders. He escorted her out and into the car without touching
her, or even glancing at her until she temporarily emerged
from her desperate anxiety to remember, 'Oh, could you make
sure that the kitchen window's open before we go, so that
Koshka can get out when she needs to—there's plenty of
water and dry food down but no litter box inside…'

With a curse and a black look of angry incredulity, he got
out of the car again with violent, jerky movements and
slammed into the house. When he came back he jammed the
key into the ignition and grimly started to drive.

Wrapped up in her pain and fear for her baby, and the bitter
knowledge that her sins of omission had caught up with her,
totally damning her in her lover's eyes, Kate hugged herself in
silent despair until Drake's question pierced her mental anguish.

'How pregnant are you?' he asked with ferocious reluctance, the words seemingly torn from deep in his chest.

'I think about eight or nine weeks by now—'

'You think? What does your doctor say?'

She didn't want to tell him she hadn't seen a doctor yet.
She knew her GP didn't handle pregnancies so she would have
to ask him to recommend a specialist or midwife as her lead
carer. She hadn't been ready to take any of those official
steps—not until she herself had felt ready to accept the giant
changes that it would immediately bring to her life.

'I—it must have happened just before you left—'

'*Happened?* A pregnancy doesn't just *happen* when you take the kind of serious precautions we do! At least I *thought* we were both on the same page about contraception. When did you stop taking the pill?'

She had known he would accuse her of trying to trap him, but it was still a blow. 'I *didn't*—not until I missed my period the week you left, and the pregnancy test came up positive… *twice*,' she emphasised, twisting to look at him and biting her lip against another sharp spasm of pain. 'I might have occasionally missed taking a pill, but never deliberately, and you always use condoms, so tell me how I could have planned this. And why would I, knowing how you feel about children—?'

'You don't know how I *feel*,' he said scathingly. 'You only think you do. But you made a big mistake if you thought you could talk me round. You're not going to con me into bearing the responsibility for *your* decision—'

She felt as if he had stabbed her in the chest. 'If you're talking about a decision not to terminate, I don't need anyone else to take responsibility for that,' she said sharply. 'I don't care what you or my mother say, I'm not getting rid of my baby just because it doesn't fit the image of a sophisticated career woman.'

He stiffened at the wheel. 'Your mother told you to have an abortion?' He cast her a violent look. But was he any better?

'I haven't told her—I wanted you to know first,' she said, turning her head to stare blindly out the window. 'But I know that's what she'll say I should do. She would have aborted me, if she could have done it legally…even back then she was thinking ahead to what would best serve her professional reputation. I grew up in a one-parent family so I know how tough it can be, but I can do it, I could even afford a house and take in boarders to help with the mortgage and child-care if necessary. There are always plenty of overseas university students looking for quality long-term home-stays. My mother will be furious and scathingly disappointed in me, but then that's nothing new…'

The thick, condemning silence descended again, reinforcing Drake's message of brutal uninterest, and this time it lasted until they arrived at the group practice on the outskirts of Whitianga. While Drake parked the car Kate walked inside and explained matters to the practice nurse on the desk, who immediately said she'd show her into an examination room to await the first doctor to become free. As she was leading the way across the hall Drake came striding up to them, eyes raking over Kate, and the nurse hesitated.

'Oh! Does your hus—um…your partner want to come in, too?'

'No!' said Kate firmly, before Drake could open his mouth to say anything hurtful. 'And he's not my partner. He just gave me a lift. You can stay in the waiting room,' she told him with dismissive coldness that blew directly off the frozen wastes in her heart.

She was feeling both hot and cold fifteen minutes later as she stared at the kindly, middle-aged female doctor in a mixture of anger and disbelief.

'But the test was positive both times I did it,' she repeated, 'and it said on the packet that it was ninety-seven per cent accurate.'

The doctor shrugged. 'Done correctly, yes, but there are a number of things that could give a false-positive result—for instance you may have let the test sit too long before you read it, or, if it happened twice, the kit might have been expired or faulty, or if you'd had a urinary-tract infection you were unaware of at the time, that could have compromised the test—'

'But I've also had all the signs since then,' protested Kate. 'I've missed two periods, and I've been nauseous, and having to go to the toilet more frequently, and my breasts have been sore…'

The doctor's voice was gentle, but inexorably firm. 'Well, I've done the internal exam and tested your urine and you're definitely not pregnant. The pain you're feeling is probably a pulled muscle from your fall, or possibly a little tear—an anti-inflammatory will soon settle that down. I'll do the hCG blood test for you but I'm sure that'll just confirm my diagnosis. You said there was some spotting a couple of weeks after your first period was due? You could have had what we call a chemical pregnancy, which is a very early miscarriage.'

'But I missed another period after that and—and I was so *sure*…'

'Have you been under any emotional stress at work or in your private life recently?'

'Well, yes, but no more than usual.' Kate grimaced. She had always found Drake's arrivals and departures very stressful—trying to act normal and carry off the appearance of cool acceptance of his wanderings while she was dying inside. Whenever he left she would wonder when they would see each other again, and when he returned she was never certain how long he would stay.

'You wanted this baby very much, I take it?' the doctor murmured, as she gently dealt with the splinters embedded in the hand with which Kate had grabbed at the rail.

'Yes,' Kate whispered. 'I did.' As soon as she had watched that test strip change she had eagerly embraced the miracle, the long-forbidden hope. She had wanted Drake's baby more than anything else in the world…except his love…

And now she had to face life with neither.

'Well, sometimes, when we want or believe in something very, very much the mind can cause the body to produce signs and symptoms that can fool a woman into thinking she's pregnant...'

Fool! Kate repeated to herself as she left the doctor's office, hollowed out by grief and the shameful knowledge of her own devastating self-betrayal.

She knew now why she had convinced herself there was no rush to have her pregnancy professionally confirmed. At some deep level of her subconscious she had known the truth and not wanted to face it. The phantom pregnancy had been a way for her to break out of the prison of her 'no strings' affair with Drake, to force herself to take action and challenge the very nature and balance of their relationship.

To make a horrible situation worse, when she got back out to the reception desk she found that she had left her purse lying on the floor back at the house, and had to ask Drake to pay for her consultation.

'Well?' he said curtly as they walked to the door.

She swallowed. She wasn't going to parade her guilt and shame in front of a roomful of interested patients. 'Quite well.' She stretched her mouth into a meaningless smile. 'The doctor said I must have pulled a muscle in my fall.'

Drake stopped outside the doors. 'So the baby's all right, then—it wasn't hurt?' he said, his voice tight with hostility at having to ask.

Kate's dry eyes ached. *Fool!* She lifted her chin. 'It was all a stupid false alarm,' she forced herself to confess.

'In that case, here.' Drake stunned her by slapping her car keys into her hand.

'You want *me* to drive home?'

'I don't care where you go. As long as I'm not there. I can't do this. I'm out of here.' He turned on his heel and headed along the pavement towards the township.

'But— I have to explain— We need to talk—' she called after him.

'No, we don't. There's nothing you could say that I want to hear. Anyway, they say actions speak louder than words.'

And with that he walked away.

CHAPTER NINE

KATE was building a sandcastle on the beach when the little girl whose lopsided lump she was busy turning into a fairy-tale structure complete with flying flags of fuzzy pussy-willow grass suddenly popped her thumb out of her mouth and extended it in a skywards spike.

'Man!'

Kneeling in the hard-packed sand just below the high-water line, Kate squinted against the low angle of the sun in the direction indicated by the moppet's soggy salute and sat back on her bare heels with a little breathless grunt of shock.

Drake was back!

Her sandy fingers unknowingly clenched, scrunching a hole in the side of a tower and endangering the route of the heroic fairy prince she had been explaining to the child was about to clamber up to rescue the enchanted maiden, aka a pod of seaweed whose green hair owed its inspiration to Rapunzel.

'Hah!' Her little companion seemed to think it was all part of a new game, and cheerfully bashed down another of Kate's painstakingly crafted towers with its pretty mosaic of shells.

'Oh, no, darling, we're building them up, not pushing them down,' choked Kate, hastily blinking away the tears she blamed on the needle-sharp jab of the sun and spreading out her hands to protect the flank of her castle from an enthusiastic little fist.

The man, who had been padding steadily along the beach towards them, came to a halt at the edge of the shallow moat on the seaward side of the castle, crouching down to survey the damage, his knees splayed, the dark trousers that had been rolled up to his calves pulling tight across the tops of his thighs, his long bare feet melting into the wet sand.

'Looks like you could do with some help,' he said, pushing up the sleeves of his pale grey knitted-silk sweater, revealing the golden brown hair on his tanned forearms.

'No, thanks, we're doing fine without you,' said Kate, just as another tower got a smashing makeover, sending a spray of damp sand into her mouth and down the top of her scoop-necked top.

'Hey, sweetheart, how about you and I fill this bucket with some more sand?' said Drake, picking up the bright plastic pail with its turret-shaped base lying by his feet and holding out the matching spade.

To Kate's disgust the little girl trotted obediently over to his side and began digging, while Drake scooped up mounds of sand with his cupped hands and rapidly filled the pail.

'You'll get your clothes dirty,' said Kate sourly, wiping the grit from her mouth with her arm, noting that it definitely wasn't beachwear he was sporting. Who had he dressed to impress? she wondered.

'Like yours?' he said, his mouth curving as he looked at her sand-clogged striped top and water-stained shorts.

When she didn't smile back, his own faded, his brown eyes unflinching as he weathered her wintry stare.

'It'll all come out in the wash,' he commented, sinking down onto his knees and turning his attention back to his task,

smoothing over the compacted sand in the bucket and invert-
ing it to produce a smooth-sided release from the bucket with
a sharp rap on the top, far more perfect than Kate had obtained.

The little girl clapped her hands.

'More!'

Drake obliged until there was another square of perfect
towers, which he joined up with mounded walls. Kate
doggedly worked on the original castle as he and his helper
dug a moat and filled it with buckets of sea water.

'I think I need to hire a decorator,' he said to Kate, noticing
her sneaking sidelong glances at the expansive grey walls.
'Would you like to help?' He picked up a single strand of
pussy willow from the bunch of grasses she had gathered in
the sand-dunes earlier and held it out to her, the delicate, pale
golden catkin at the end of the stalk quivering and dancing in
the gentle sea breeze.

It was too reminiscent of an extended olive branch and she
opened her mouth to coldly refuse, but then she saw the girl's
innocent blue eyes, alight with eagerness, fixed on her face.

She reached out to reluctantly accept the offering.

'I suppose I could.' Her voice was like broken glass but the
little girl listened to the words, not the jagged tone, and as
Kate poked the stalk into the top of one of the new towers she
began pulling her precious collection of shells from the
sagging pocket of her shorts and handing them over one by
one for Kate to press into the base of the walls.

Watching her crawling around on her hands and knees,
Drake said with a curious edge, 'Should you be doing that?
What about your pulled muscle?'

She didn't understand his concern. After all, he had been
the one to turn his back on her grief-stricken admission. He
must have realised how shocked and upset she was, how dev-

astated by her humiliating mistake. He hadn't cared *then* what she was going through.

'The doctor gave me an anti-inflammatory. The pain relief was pretty well immediate.'

He frowned. 'Don't those things have harmful side-effects?'

'I'm sure the doctor wouldn't have prescribed it if it was dangerous,' Kate told him tartly. 'But if you were so worried about it perhaps you should have asked me about it at the time instead of running off like that. But then, that's fairly typical behaviour for you, isn't it?'

She hadn't meant to let that slip out, but when she saw the skin tauten over his cheekbones she was glad. There was no reason now to hold back, no secret baby to protect. She was on her own.

'Oh, yes, that's a pretty one, isn't it, darling?' she said as the little girl poked a small paua shell with its pearlised blue and green interior under her nose.

'Here, Kristin, put it in your bucket,' said Drake, handing it over with the spade tucked inside, startling Kate with his use of the girl's name.

'You know who she is?'

'Of course I do, they're locals. Look, Kristin—your mother's getting ready to take you back up for your tea.'

The woman whom Kate had briefly spoken to earlier had repacked her beach bag and was shaking out her towel. Seeing them looking towards her, she waved, yelled out a greeting to Drake and her thanks to Kate, and called to her daughter, who skipped off without a second glance at the result of all their hard work when she heard the words 'spaghetti' and 'ice cream' floating on the breeze.

'There's gratitude for you,' murmured Drake as she got stiffly to her feet. 'Never mind, the tide's still on its way out and the local school kids should be getting off the bus about now. Your monument will get plenty of admiration before the sea comes back to demolish it. Here…' He sought and found a stick from amongst the heaps of seaweed strewn along the high watermark and wrote 'Kate and Kristin did this' in large capitals alongside the crenellated towers.

Kate found it interesting that he had added the little girl's name without prompting, but not his own.

'For someone who doesn't want any children, I'm surprised you're so good at handling them,' she said, unable to curb her resentment. 'Most people who haven't had much contact with children find it hard to relate to them.'

Herself included. She had never been interested in babies or young children until she had thought she was pregnant, then they had turned out to be the subject of a profound, and hitherto inadmissible fascination. Again she felt that deep, wrenching sorrow, the sense of loss that she had no right to feel. She began to walk quickly back along the beach towards the house.

Drake had tensed at her words. 'In the kind of group homes I was in there are always plenty of kids coming and going.' He shrugged, turning to follow her, easily keeping up with her swinging strides. 'It's supposed to be part of the "family experience" to get the teenagers to help look after the younger ones.'

His voice petered out, as if he expected her to interrupt with a question, but Kate merely quickened her pace, the breeze against her face making her eyes sting as she pulled ahead.

'I came back, didn't I?' he said roughly, digging his feet into the sand to regain her shoulder. 'That must count for something.'

'You think?' she said sarcastically.

'I was only gone a couple of days.'

Eternity times two. He was very efficient at his disappearing act, though, for he had even arranged for a man in a pick-up to come and collect Prince and lock up the house. When Kate had seen that happening she had wished that falling in hate was as easy as falling in love. At least she had still had Koshka to stroke and to hold, and to lick away her tears. The little cat had slept on her bed, curled up on the turndown of the sheet, her soft motoring purr a comforting reassurance that Kate had not been left entirely alone in the world.

'Yes, that's quite a record turn-around for you. I thought you'd be away much longer,' she said truthfully. 'But I forgot that you have a work in progress. You had to come back for that—you have a lot of writing to do. And of course that always takes precedence over everything else!' She could hear herself getting shrill and was relieved to see her front lawn. She almost broke into a run.

'Kate— That's not why I came back.' He leapt up on the grass and shadowed her to the scene of her fall. 'I only went as far as Craemar—the Marlows' holiday place—Steve put me up there—'

'Oh, I see, and I suppose you told him all about me,' she said with one foot on the step. 'Cried into your beer and gave chapter and verse on how I almost tricked you into having to behave like an ordinary human being—'

'God, Kate, *no*,' he said, snagging the sleeve of her top to hold her back, 'it wasn't like that—his whole family were there—'

She had thought her humiliation was complete; now she discovered there was fresh reason to cringe. 'You mean *they* all know about it, now, too?' she cried in horror.

'I haven't told *anyone*, Kate. I didn't go there to get drunk and rave; I just needed to get away to *think*.'

She pulled her sleeve out of his grasp. She didn't know what to believe any more. She didn't trust him—or herself—

to know what was really true. 'Excuse me, I think I'm going to go inside and be sick,' she flung at him, and rushed up the stairs, hoping that would be enough to make him think twice about harassing her with his unwanted attention.

Unfortunately her words had the opposite effect and after scarcely a moment of hesitation he charged into the house behind her, following her trail of sandy footprints right into the sanctuary of her bedroom where she had fled to shed bitter tears.

'What are you doing in here?' she said thickly, backing away from him, glad that she hadn't yet succumbed to the building pressure behind her eyes.

'You said you were going to be sick.'

Just as the doctor had predicted they would, the physical symptoms of her pregnancy had vanished, so she couldn't blame her savage burst of fury on a hormonal mood swing.

'And you wanted to what? Enjoy watching my misery?'

'I thought you might need some help.'

She was infuriated by his strained gentleness. 'You haven't been much help so far—why start now?'

'Calm down, Kate, it isn't good for you to get all wrought up over trifles.'

Trifles? Kate's mouth fell open at his sheer gall.

He looked around the room, which was in a defiant mess very different from her normal, fastidious requirements, and frowned.

'Are you packing?'

She recovered from her momentary speechlessness. 'You wish! Unlike you I don't choose to run away from my problems.' No, she ran *to* them. That was *her* problem!

'Then what's all this?' He nudged a foot against a stack of carrier bags by the door.

'Just some things of mine I'm putting out for the rubbish.'

One of the packages slumped, spilling out books, and he bent to tuck them back in the bag, jerking upright as if he had been burnt when he saw the colourful titles.

'You're throwing out your books on child-care?'

She gave a bitter laugh at his fierce frown. 'Well, I won't need them now, will I? Do you think I should give them away to charity? Feel free to take as many as you like.'

His body took on a dangerous lean. 'What do you mean you won't need them, now?' he said warily.

He wasn't usually so obtuse. 'Well, if I'm not going to be a parent, I don't need to read books on how to develop good parenting skills,' she choked.

Did he think she would want to keep the reminders of her foolishness around for next time she thought she was pregnant? She was twenty-seven, and in love with a man who had brutally rejected the very essence of her womanhood—at this rate there would never be a 'next time'.

His wariness gave way to stark tension. 'What are you going to do? Give the baby up for adoption?'

Kate gasped, shaking her head helplessly.

His face greyed. 'God, you haven't decided to go for a termination after all?' He heeled his chest with his hand, as if massaging the flood flow through his heart. 'Kate, you're not thinking straight. You can't abort your baby...you'll never be able to live with yourself. It's not the right decision for you—'

He didn't know!

Kate stood frozen, inwardly reeling with shock.

He didn't know there was no baby! She'd thought he had understood—outside the clinic when she'd told him it was all a false alarm—she had thought he'd realised that she meant the whole pregnancy. But he had obviously thought she meant the threatened miscarriage!

He still thought that she was pregnant.

And he didn't want her to abort his baby.

No, not *his*...'your baby', he said, not 'my baby' or 'our baby'. He was firmly separating mother and child from any connection with himself.

'But it is my decision,' she said cruelly. 'Unless you want to go to court and fight over the right to the foetus—drag out our past, present and future for the world to gloat over...'

He flinched, but stood his ground, the muscles grinding along his jaw. 'Kate, don't make any decisions on the basis of the hurt and anger you're feeling right now. Believe me, I know how badly that goes—how irrevocable some acts of bitterness can be. Every life is precious, because life is so fleeting we have to treasure it while we can...I came back because you're important to me, and this baby doesn't change that.'

Again, it was 'this baby' not 'his', thought Kate, growing icier with every word.

'The fact that it was unplanned by either of us doesn't have to be a disaster.'

So he was prepared to concede that she hadn't tried to trap him with the oldest trick in the book. How generous!

'I'm a wealthy man, I can set up a trust fund to support you and the baby for the rest of your lives, so there'll be plenty of money for child-care if you want to continue your career.'

Ah, there it was, the pay-off!

'And we can buy you a house, one with plenty of room that you won't have to share.' He was growing uncharacteristically nervous at her silence, speaking more quickly and persuasively. 'It'll be much more convenient than your town house and more private than my hotel—no need to be self-conscious if you ask me to stay overnight...'

If? That big, fat, horribly pregnant 'if' sent a huge chunk of fractured ice shearing off her glacial heart.

Now he was prepared to take on her and the baby, albeit stashed in an expensive love-nest somewhere? Now, when it no longer mattered! If he had once mentioned love instead of ticking off his convenient boxes she might have reacted differently, but this was too little and too late.

She marched out of the bedroom and threw open the front door in a furious gesture of repudiation.

'Get out!'

'Kate, I'm only trying to make you see—'

'Get *out* of my house!' She would have liked to have told him that she wanted him to never darken her door again, but as well as being horridly clichéd it would have been a lie.

He hesitated and she thought that if he pointed out that it wasn't actually her house she would hit him, but fortunately he brushed past her, turning on the doorstep to warn her.

'OK, I'm going—but I'm not going away, Kate. Not again. And you're not leaving Oyster Beach, either, until we work things through. Sooner or later you and I are going to have to deal with the consequences of our actions—*together*, rather than individually. Our baby is as much a part of me as it is of you, because, after two years, *you're* part of me...'

He couldn't have said anything more calculated to play on her conscience.

After vowing to be honest in all her future dealings with him she had just been vindictive and cruel. She had let him go away thinking she was holding his baby hostage in her barren womb.

Kate paced the house as the sun sank lower in the sky, running her hands constantly through her hair, as if she could brush away the sticky tendrils of guilt clinging to her mind and disordering her thoughts. She couldn't stomach the idea of food, but since her strange cravings and loathings had vanished with the baby she made herself a good, strong, black and bitter cup of instant caffeine.

Taking her coffee out to the verandah, she couldn't help glance wistfully up at Drake's shuttered office window. The light was on and the shutters were slanted open, a motionless black silhouette standing, staring down at her through the tilted slats, a lonely, brooding figure who sent a hot needle of pain searing through the ice encasing her emotions.

A boy who had been abandoned by his father, suffered the ultimate fatal rejection from his mother; shadowed by a teenager who had been bounced from pillar to post in foster care; shaded by a man who had never had—or permitted—anybody but a mangy dog to possess a piece of his soul. How could she condemn him to mental torture for merely being the product of his environment?

Leaving her half-finished coffee steaming on the kitchen table, Kate put a bowl of canned cat-food down for Koshka and walked around to Drake's front door.

Her knock was answered so quickly she realised he must have seen her coming. She also realised that she was still barefooted and wearing the sandy, salty clothes she had worn to the beach whereas Drake had obviously not been brooding so hard that he hadn't taken the time to shower and shave, and change into clean jeans and a short-sleeved white linen shirt.

'Come in,' he said, his deep voice quiet and inviting as he stepped back and to one side, but she didn't move.

'There is no baby.' She could hardly hear herself over the thunder of her heart in her ears.

'I beg your pardon?' He greeted her bald announcement

with a puzzled tilt of his head, as if he thought he hadn't heard her correctly.

'I'm not having a baby. That doctor confirmed it. I'm not pregnant. That's what I meant when I told you it was a false alarm.' She lifted her chin when she saw a red flare in his eyes, an instant before they turned as black as pitch. 'So you see, you can stop worrying—there are no consequences for us to deal with after all,' she continued in a steady monotone. 'I just came over to tell you that—'

'Oh, no, you didn't,' said Drake, grabbing her around the waist as she turned to leave. He hauled her inside the door and slammed it shut, engaging the dead-bolt.

His arms caged her against the door on either side of her sun-flushed shoulders, his face a series of jagged angles under the flare of the overhead light in the vaulted entranceway, his velvet voice as abrasive as sandpaper in his bewilderment.

'I don't understand. Explain it to me, Kate. Are you saying the initial test was *wrong*? And that your own doctor never noticed?'

So she was forced to drag it out, to tell him all the gory, embarrassing details that had been picked over by the doctor in Whitianga, including the damning fact that she had never consulted her own doctor.

Mired in her guilt, she waited stoically for a celebratory cheer of relief, followed by a justifiable outburst of anger and contempt, but Drake's response was so muted it could have been called a non-response.

'So you *could* have been pregnant a few weeks ago, but we'll never really know,' he said quietly when she had mentioned the chemical pregnancy theory.

She shrugged, her bare shoulder blades rubbing against the

wood of the door. 'The doctor said that apparently around half of first pregnancies end in a miscarriage, sometimes so early that the woman doesn't even know about it.'

'But *you* knew,' he said, dropping his arms and straightening up.

'I *thought* I knew,' she said, free to move past him into the big, unlit living area where she could safely avoid his all-seeing gaze. Someone had lit a bonfire at the far end of the beach and through the big picture windows she could see the fiery sparks leaping up into the sky, reaching out for the cool sprawl of stars that were just beginning to prick through as dusk teetered on the edge of night. 'As it turns out I was only pretending…'

'I'm sorry.' His voice was soft as the night as he came up behind her.

The breath shivered out of her lungs and she wrapped her arms around herself, wishing she were one of those sparks, dancing up into nothingness. 'Why? You never wanted the baby—'

'Not for the baby. For you. For *your* loss. Because it was so much more than a pretence for you, wasn't it, Kate? For weeks you thought you were having my baby…'

She bit her lip, but the self-inflicted pain didn't help banish the tears that stood in her eyes, blurring the dance of the sparks. She opened them wide and blinked, but then a strong pair of enfolding arms slid around and over hers, chasing away the chill, drawing her gently back against a warm column of hard flesh, and the tears spilled over her cheeks and dripped down into the crease of a tanned elbow.

The arms tightened and she felt Drake's square chin skim over her shoulder at the nape of her neck, his head dipping and turning so that he could push his face into the side of her throat, his hard forehead nudging up under her jaw, his lips moving against her soft skin.

'Ah, Katherine…I'm sorry…' He began to rock her from side to side, his big hands compressing her upper arms, his hips directing but also passively supporting the sway of her willowy body.

A sob burst from her chest and she briefly struggled against his unbreakable grip.

'Kate…' he whispered against her throat. 'Katie…'

It was the first time he had ever used the sweet diminutive of her name and that he should do it now just seemed too much. A second sob tore loose, and then another, and then the tears just wouldn't stop. When she stopped fighting his hold he slid his arms down to her hips and turned her around, pulling her hands around his waist, drawing her head against his chest and rubbing the knuckles of one hand up and down her spine, continuing to rock her in rhythm to her sobs.

'I don't know why I'm crying; there's nothing to cry about,' she wept, her voice muffled in the folds of his linen shirt. 'It's not as if I've really lost a baby…just a silly delusion… What made me think I could be a good mother, anyway? I suppose you think I'm totally mad—'

'Shh, Kate,' he soothed, 'you're the sanest woman I know—you're the one who anchors *me* to my humanity.' He rested his cheek on the top of her tousled head. 'You lost something precious to you this week, and even if it *was* just an illusion, why shouldn't you be allowed to grieve for it?'

Her fingers clenched into his shirt, the beat of his heart against her jaw reverberating through her bones. 'You don't really care,' she choked, lifting her head. 'You're happy that your life can go back to the way it was before…'

'Not happy…sad.' He tilted her chin up so that she could

see the truth of his words in his sombre face. 'In all the time I've known you I've never seen you cry, except at a movie. That made me feel safe. I don't like to see you hurting.'

She looked up at him with drowned eyes, a ghostly silver in the half-darkness. 'Then *why*… why did you walk away from me like that?' she said rawly.

He brushed back the hair from her forehead, dislodging several grains of sand, which he stroked away from the top of her furrowed brows. 'Because I'm a flawed human being, sweetheart. Sometimes I let the past get in the way of my better instincts. But I do learn from my mistakes and I'm here for you now, so you don't have to bear this alone.'

He pressed his lips to her crumpled forehead, smoothing it out with a string of gentle kisses that drifted to the corner of her damp eyes, and down to her salty cheeks and bite-swollen lips. His soft murmurs of tender reassurance and the rocking cradle of his arms, the feather-light touch of his mouth stroking her reddened eyelids closed, and the achingly sweet brush of his cheek against hers both lulled and enticed her into a dreamy state of contented acquiescence.

So that when she found herself upstairs in Drake's luxurious grey and blue bedroom, being divested of her clothes, she was only mildly curious.

'What are you doing?' she murmured through tear-thickened vocal cords as Drake's comforting arms withdrew so that he could pick up a remote control to draw the blue silk drapes and dim the squat bedside lamps to an intimate glow.

'Getting comfortable,' he said, pulling the white shirt over his head without undoing the buttons, and discarding it carelessly on the thick silver-grey carpet. He did the same with her top and was deftly drawing her salt-stained shorts down her legs when she bestirred herself to weakly protest.

'I haven't had a wash. You can't look at me; I'm all grubby—'

'I don't mind. Hop out,' he ordered and threw the shorts on top of the pile of clothes when she unthinkingly obeyed.

'I do. I always have a shower before I see you,' she fretted, trying to hide herself behind her arms. 'I need to feel that I'm clean, and look my best, and smell beautiful…'

He took her hands, gently saluting the one that still showed signs of bruising from the extracted splinters, and placed them over his shoulders, spanning her slender waist with his big hands and nuzzling her pouting mouth with more of those butterfly kisses. 'You're just as appealing to me au naturel,' he murmured reassuringly. 'You smell like a real woman; I like that better than any artificial fragrance…a woman of the sun and sea and beach.'

He licked at the tracks of her tears on her face and she gave a sad, salty chuckle.

'You feel like Koshka, only your tongue is softer.'

He gave her some more of his soft tongue, and took advantage of her distraction to unfasten her bra, letting out an exclamation as a thick crust of dry sand fell away with the cups, leaving her bare breasts coated with a fine dusting of pale grit, the minute grains of quartz sparkling in the lamp-light.

'I need a towel, I'm all sandy,' she said self-consciously, wrinkling her nose and trying to ineffectually brush away the grittiness.

'Fairy dust from your fairy castle,' he said huskily. 'Here, let me be your towel…' He replaced her hands on his shoulders and used the tips of his fingers to whisk delicately over and around the soft mounds, stroking his thumbs where the sand clung stubbornly to her milk-white flesh. He bent his head to blow gently at the recalcitrant grains, watching her breasts rise and tauten, the soft pink nipples puckering at the caress of the warm, moist zephyr. He pushed her to sit on the bed and picked up his shirt, kneeling in front to her to tenderly buff around the ruched peaks with the butter-soft linen, his eyes darkening as she flinched and gave a sudden gasp.

'Oh, a button.'

He looked at the balled shirt in his hand, its pearlised buttons gleaming amongst the folds of fabric. 'Did it catch against you?'

She nodded.

'Like this…?' He deliberately turned the shirt and scraped a smooth, hard button against her sensitised nipple.

'Oh…' She shuddered, her eyes widening, her head tipping back, and he did it again, scraping the little disc back and forth across the swollen peak until it deepened from pink to mauve, then according the same delicious punishment to her other breast.

'Oh…they…oh, don't,' she gasped unconvincingly as the blood thinned in her veins, rushing into her breasts and pooling between her thighs, easing her sorrowing heart of some of its coagulated heaviness. She closed her eyes and groaned, racked by a piercing yearning.

'They're almost clean now,' she heard him murmur throatily. 'I just need to…' and suddenly the fabric was replaced by his warm breath again, and then his mouth, licking around her areolae, suckling gently but firmly at the twin peaks.

'Would you have nursed our baby like this?'

Her eyes flew open with shock to meet his hot gaze, smouldering at her through his thick lashes, his lips still drawing tautly on her nipple, enfolding it inside his mouth in the hot curl of his tongue.

She plunged her hand into his hair and pulled his head away. 'How can you ask that?'

He looked at her pointed breasts, cleansed of sand but glistening with the evidence of his possession. 'I don't want you to be afraid to talk about it. I don't want you to think you have to pretend it never happened. You would have been a good mother, Kate, never doubt it.'

The reminder made her feel guilty all over again. 'We shouldn't be doing this…'

'But it's making you feel better, isn't it?'

She quivered with confusion. 'I'm not going to have sex with you,' she said fiercely. Men always reduced everything to sex!

'All right…we'll just get into bed and cuddle together—you'd like that, wouldn't you?' he suggested persuasively, reaching over to fold back a corner of the blue silk counterpane and show her the crisp white sheet. 'You'd never let us do that before. You'd allow the requisite few minutes for a post-coital cuddle, but as soon as there was any danger of either of us drifting off to sleep you'd be up and moving about, suggesting things to do or getting dressed to leave.'

'I thought that was what you wanted…' she said, bewildered and intrigued by this seductively tender alien who had apparently taken over Drake's body.

'Well, you were wrong. I like having you close. I wanted to make love *and* be able to fall asleep to the feel of you in my arms.' His eyes had fallen to her filmy white lace panties, and his finger began to toy with the elastic at the top of her leg.

She clamped her legs together to halt a molten gush. What if he found sand in her panties?

'I'm not taking them off…' she said weakly.

His finger hooked under the fabric. 'I think you should,' he advised. In contrast to hers his deep voice was compellingly certain. 'They're a bit tight, and you want to be comfy…' And before she could blink, or accuse him of calling her fat, they were whisking through the air.

'All right, but you have to keep your jeans on,' she warned, her white bottom flashing as she scrabbled hastily under the covers and peeped out at him, using the sheet to cover the beginnings of a smile.

He looked disappointed but contented himself with merely unsnapping his top button to relieve the pressure behind his zip.

He climbed into the bed facing her, snuggling tantalisingly—but not crushingly—close, his hot chest just far enough away to rub her breasts with every indrawn breath, his big hands stroking her back, his heavy thigh lying over the top of hers, the centres of their bodies pressed together, the springy curls at the base of her belly catching against the rough denim bulging tightly in his crotch.

Their heads nestled on thistledown softness, their noses almost touching at the sloping intersection of their luxury pillows.

'This is nice, isn't it?' he said, one hand moving down to cup the globes of her bottom, adjusting her more securely against his lower body, and she felt his voice in the hard tips of her breasts where they fenced with his flat nipples.

'Y-yes…' she said uncertainly, feeling the familiar throb of excitement pulse in her veins.

The longer she lay there, the worse it got. She didn't want him to want her only for sex, she realised restlessly, but their thriving sex life was a healthy expression of their intense mutual attraction, and, as such, was an indivisible part of her love.

As her temperature rose she could feel his skin absorb and radiate more heat until it began to get uncomfortably hot under the covers. And yet still he made no move to acknowledge or ease the growing tension in their bodies. In spite of his earlier seductiveness, Drake was going to refrain from any sexualised affection because she had insisted she wanted it that way. He was showing that he respected her wishes above his carnal desires, when what she really wanted was not re-straint, but reckless proof of life.

Kate impatiently kicked off the smothering covers. 'You can make love to me now.'

Drake reared up on his elbow. 'Are you sure?' he asked tensely.

She dug her nails into his arms impatiently. 'Yes, I'm sure…Drake, I want you—I want you to make love to me here, *now*!'

He didn't need a third invitation. Nor was there any long-drawn-out foreplay. He tossed off the covers and swivelled them sideways on the bed, tugging her hips to the edge of the mattress, sliding backwards until his feet struck the floor. Propping himself over her on one braced arm, he opened the fastening of his jeans and pushed himself deeply inside her, uttering a thick, guttural sound of satisfaction as she lifted her hips to guide him home. With a twisting jerk of his hips he seated himself even more tightly between her spread legs, the muscles in his thighs rippling under the denim as he braced his feet against the floor, bent his hungry mouth to her breasts, and began the deep, hard, thrusting rhythm that they both urgently needed, bringing them quickly to a mutual, violent convulsion of groaning ecstasy.

Twice more he racked and then wrenched her body with convulsive pleasure before turning off the lights and finish-ing with a long, slow, sensual loving that left them panting and weak with sweet exhaustion. Then he pulled the sheets firmly back around them, arranged her to his satisfac-tion…facing away from him with her bottom spooned by his hips…and tucked his arms around her, sealing her back to his smooth chest.

'And now,' he informed her with yawning satisfaction, 'now we cuddle up and go to sleep together like all good lovers do!'

CHAPTER TEN

Two weeks later, Kate tiptoed up the hall to stand outside the firmly shut door to Drake's office, pressing a warning finger to her lips as she looked down at Prince, trailing at her heels, who looked to be winding up for an inquiring 'wuff'.

She raised a hand to knock and dropped it again, chewing at her lip. The door shut meant that Drake wasn't to be disturbed—they had arranged that all-important signal right from the start. If she came over and his door was shut, she went away again.

Except in dire emergencies. Which this wasn't—well, not as Drake would class it, anyway...

'I can hear you thinking!'

Muffled by the near soundproof door, Drake's voice made her jump.

'Woof!' yelled Prince at the sound of his master's voice, clearly letting her off the hook. Or so she thought.

'You may as well come in, Kate.'

She cracked the door open and poked her head in, pushing Prince back with a firm hand.

'I wasn't going to knock,' she told him. 'I was going to wait. Have I wrecked your train of thought?'

He angled his head down and looked at her over the top of

his narrow spectacles. She had been charmed to discover that he wore the neat, gold-rimmed reading glasses when he worked for prolonged periods at his desk. She had teased him that it made him look like a 'proper writer', but he had got her back by wearing them the next time they made love, and forcing her to admit that they made him look incredibly sexy.

'Do you want the polite answer, or the truth?'

'The polite answer, please,' she said, pushing the door wider.

He threw down the gold-topped pen with which he had been correcting pages and took off his glasses.

'You're looking rather frazzled.'

'I'm frizzled *and* frazzled,' she said, fingering through her salt-laden locks. I don't seem to have any water.'

'Low tide classified as an emergency now, is it?' he asked, but his brown eyes were amused as he rocked back in his chair, lazily stretching his arms before tucking his hands behind his head. 'If you wait twelve hours I'm sure it'll come back in again.'

'I mean at the house. I went to have a shower and nothing happened. None of the taps are working, either. The rental agent said to phone a plumber, but apparently he doesn't work weekends in Oyster Beach…unless you have too *much* water. He'll come for a flood but not a drought. Would you mind if I used your guest shower?'

He gave her an impatient look. 'You know you don't have to even ask, you can shower here whenever you like—or have a soak in the spa.' His eyes glinted. 'I know you like a long, leisurely bathe, so that your skin is soft when you stroke on those silky body lotions.'

He was reminding her that more than once he had applied them for her, revealing a wicked talent for erotic massage…

'Thanks,' she said in an effort to stay focused on her errand.

'I've been down on the beach all morning and I think I've brought half of it back with me.'

He looked approvingly at her glowing colour. 'Aren't you glad I persuaded Marcus to give you an extra month's holiday?'

'Persuaded? Blackmailed, more like!' she laughed.

Impossible to believe now that she had initially rejected Drake's suggestion that she spend a few more leisurely weeks at the beach, but he had been very persuasive and hadn't hesitated to use her area of greatest vulnerability.

'You've just gone through a very emotionally draining experience; you owe it to yourself to fully recover before you plunge back into the fray,' he had lectured. 'Didn't the doctor say something about your stress levels helping to send your hormones all out of whack? Marcus will work you into a nervous breakdown if you're not careful. I know he regards you highly but that doesn't mean you should let him persuade you that you're completely indispensable—that's just his way of cracking the whip and making least-work for himself. Another month isn't too much to ask when you've worked for him continuously for so long, and your health is at stake. I bet you've hardly had a day of sick leave in your whole career. He owes you a long-service sabbatical at the very least—'

'Well, I suppose I could phone and ask…' she said uncertainly, tempted by the thought of a few more stolen weeks alone with her lover, and yet at the same time mistrustful of her current state of blissful irresponsibility. This was her healing time and she and Drake were consciously living it from moment to moment, taking each day as it came and carefully putting aside any reference to the future.

'Don't ask him, *tell* him!' And when she baulked at that he shrugged and seemed to give up.

But when she finally borrowed Drake's phone to make the toll-call, she found Marcus strangely affable, chuckling fatly in her ear and reassuring her that her job would be waiting for her however long she decided to stay away, that she was worth her weight in gold and that any research she wanted to do for a private client while she was away was okey-dokey with him.

'You went behind my back!' Kate confronted Drake as soon as she'd hung up the phone, trying hard to be angry.

'It was for your own good. Someone had to play hard-ball on your behalf.'

'How would you like it if I negotiated one of your contracts without telling you?' she demanded.

'Be my guest, sweetheart, I hate all that hoopla,' he drawled, taking the wind out of her sails. 'I could fire my agent and save myself twenty per cent!'

The next tussle between them was that Drake had decided it was silly for her to continue to pay her holiday rental when she was sleeping nearly every night in his bed. 'Since you're spending so much time over here you may as well stay for the next few weeks,' he tossed out casually. 'With the high season coming, I think you'll find you won't be able to renew your rental for another month, anyway.'

'I think it's better if I keep my own space. If I can't, and there isn't another rental somewhere nearby, I'll just go home,' said Kate with firm finality, her heart in her mouth as she rejected his offhand invitation. But she wasn't going to make any more life-changing decisions based on foolish assumptions. She knew all too well how dangerous wishful thinking could be, and Drake's offer had been only for her to stay, not to move in with him. There was a subtle, but enormous difference, particularly when the phrase was used by a man whose business was subtle shades of meaning.

'Besides, I know how vital your privacy is to you when you're working,' she reminded him. 'So, thanks for the offer, but it's better this way for both of us.'

Fortunately, when she contacted the rental agent, he shuffled his files and came across a note about the unexpected cancellation of his next booking, so to her relief she and Koshka were able to settle in for the duration.

'Why don't I come and see what the problem is with your water,' he said now, switching off his computer monitor and lunging out of his chair.

'But your door was shut,' she said guiltily, following him downstairs with Prince.

'And it would have stayed shut if I hadn't been stuck in a rut. A bit of he-man stuff on the side might kick something loose,' he said, fetching a few tools from his garage and stuffing them into his jeans pockets.

'Is it going badly, then?' she said sympathetically.

He gave her a slightly defensive sidelong look. 'No, actually, in general it's going rather well.'

Which was more than could be said for her shower.

'Do you know anything about plumbing?' she asked dubiously as she watched him tinker and curse at the shower head.

He bristled as if she had challenged his manhood. 'I helped build irrigation systems in the desert—what do you think?'

She threw up her hands in surrender. 'Just asking. Er…I'll leave you to it, then,' she said, hurriedly backing out of the bathroom as he pinched the skin between thumb and forefinger in the wrench and swore even more viciously.

Some time later he sought her out in the lounge, where she was reading with Koshka dozing on her lap.

'It's no use. You're not going to have water any time soon. Your pump has packed up.'

'What pump?' asked Kate, depositing the sleeping cat on the couch.

'You're on bore-water here. The pump sucks it out of the ground and then pumps it from a tank through to your pipes. It may be a major job to fix it. Even if the plumber gets onto it right straight away he'll probably have to wait for parts.'

'Oh, so what do you think I should do?'

'There's nothing you can do at the moment. You obviously can't stay here without water. Unless you fancy ferrying a bucket from next door every time you want to flush your toilet,' he added sarcastically as he watched her open her mouth to protest.

Within an hour he had her packed up and installed in the large, ground-floor bedroom at the front of his house, looking on with folded arms as she hung her clothes in the big walk-in closet.

'This is only temporary—until the pump is fixed,' said Kate, turning to place a stack of her folded underwear into the chest of drawers and catching the quiet look of satisfaction on his face.

'Of course.'

She looked at him sharply and he responded with a smile of devilish smugness. 'Well, I guess I'll be getting back to work. You know where everything is by now. Make yourself at home…'

She knew where the smugness came from when she met the laconic plumber who after several postponements was frustratingly vague on an estimate of exactly when she could expect to have running water again, and over a week later she was still totting up the amount of the refund that she would be owed by the landlord.

And loving living with Drake.

At first she was restless and edgy and very conscious of

the need not to encroach, but that feeling eased when he casually asked if she would mind doing a little research for him and she plunged eagerly into the task of combing his extensive library and using his extra laptop to pull down information from the internet on the geopolitical history of the Balkans. He was first amused by her enthusiasm, and then taken aback at the speed at which she synthesised the facts.

'This is duck-to-water stuff for you, isn't it?' he murmured when he sat down to lunch to find yet another concise fact-sheet sitting by his plate. 'This'll save me a hell of a lot of reading. I'm sorry if I've turned this into a bit of a busman's holiday for you.'

'I'm happy to sing for my supper,' she told him readily.

His brown eyes glowed. 'You do that already, in much more exciting ways.'

Colour touched her cheekbones. 'I'm glad you like my cooking,' she said primly, deliberately reading an innocent meaning into his provocative words. 'Perhaps I should be charging *you*—Marcus did suggest I might take on a private commission.'

'Maybe that's because I hinted to him that I could benefit from your expertise,' he admitted with laughter in his eyes. 'He practically fell over himself at the thought he might get a book out of me a second sooner. And if you want to hear me sing, sweetheart, you only have to touch me the way you did last night...'

She loved the nights even more than the days, and not just for the intimate dinners and excitement of his love-making, but for what came afterwards, when they would lie in each other's arms in the dark, talking.

That was when he gradually expanded on the details of his life with his mother, and the jealous possessiveness that had grown like a cancer, distorting her love into the sick obsession that destroyed her life, turning him from a son into a whipping boy for the man who bred him, and then into an enemy as he had tried to fight against her long slide into drug-addiction.

It was in the still of the night that Kate's unspoken love and serene acceptance were rewarded by the secrets of his guarded heart. He seemed to find it easier to talk in the dark and she certainly found it easier to listen.

One evening he came back from a trip to the store with a package under his arm.

'It's from Marcus,' he said, sitting on a stool at the break-fast bar to slit the large envelope and extract a note and a smaller, striped airmail envelope.

Kate froze in the act of slicing vegetables for dinner. 'I thought he didn't know where you lived?'

'He does now—at least he knows about the post box at the store,' he murmured, studying the writing on the front and the back of the envelope.

'Well, he didn't find out about it from me,' she said quickly.

'No, from me.' He glanced up and smiled ruefully at her expression. 'Part of our trade-off for your extra month: satisfying his curiosity and making myself a little less inaccessible.'

Kate was stunned. 'I thought all the arm-twisting was the other way around. And so you just *told* him?' she said, her heart swelling. 'For me?'

He shrugged as if he had dropped a damp squib rather than a bombshell. 'It was inevitable I'd tell him soon, anyway. I'm thinking of getting off the merry-go-round and moving down here permanently. Now that I have a solid backlist and financial security for life, I can concentrate more on the writing and scale back on the tours and the high-profile personal publicity.'

He was thinking of moving to Oyster Beach! Kate felt the shock of it move through her body. Where would that leave her?

'When are you thinking of moving?'

'I haven't got that far in my planning,' he said, with discouraging brevity.

Her eyes fell to the envelope he was turning over and over in his hands.

'Why don't you open it?' she asked.

'Because I know who it's from.' He tossed it down so that she could see the return address. It was from Perth, Australia.

James John Richardson.

Richardson?

She raised her eyes to his face. 'Is that—?'

He smiled grimly. 'I'm sure there's more than one James John Richardson in the world, but Marcus says that this particular one claims to be my long-lost father. He sent Enright's a letter asking for this one to be passed along.'

'Do you think he is?'

'I know he is. I made sure I always knew where the bastard was, and that he never knew who I was.'

'Are you going to read it?'

He stood up, his body stiff with rejection. 'He's nothing to me. I have no interest in communicating with him—ever.'

'But it could be important—'

'No!' He turned on his heel. 'You read it if you're so interested. I have work to do....'

Kate contemplated the envelope for a long time after he left before she picked it up and ran her knife along the flap. The letter inside was a single sheet, typed.

When she went up to his office, Drake was standing on the balcony, looking over the beach, his arms braced against the solid rail. He didn't look at her as she quietly came up beside him, the letter open in her hand.

'He wants money, of course,' he told her harshly.

She had done his research, now he needed her précis. 'He said he saw your photograph in a bookshop and knew who you were because you look just like his other sons. He did some digging and says he thinks the press would be very interested in the pitiful story he has to tell, if you won't help him out of his financial difficulties. He says you owe him for putting up with your mother's craziness long enough to have you. That you're rich enough for a few hundred grand not to make any difference to you. How did you know?'

'Because it was never going to be a letter of reconciliation and remorse.' His smile was a rictus of bitterness. 'He never had any remorse for what he did. He can rot in hell for all I care.'

'But if he sells his story—?'

'Let him,' he ground out. 'All publicity is good publicity according to Marcus—right? The scandal might even sell me a few hundred more books.'

'Drake—' She put her hand on his shoulder and he shrugged away her sympathy with a violent jerk of his body.

'My name was Michael James Richardson. I was taught to be very proud of my father, to do everything I could to be a good son. But not good enough. Because after he left my father had another son, and he christened *him* Michael James Richardson. He took even my identity from me, wiped me out as if I didn't exist. So I wiped him out. Let him bring on the world—he's getting nothing from me!'

That night, he took her with an almost painful ferociousness and afterwards, their bodies spooned together, his palm resting heavily on her belly, he told her about his little brother, Ross, who was born when he was nine.

'I don't know who the father was, but it was probably one of my mother's dealers, I suppose—she was taking everything she could by then and would do pretty much anything for a fix—or one of her coke-head friends. She claimed James had come back and wanted her to have his baby, and that made her try to clean up for a while, but it didn't last much past the birth. So I was the one who looked after Ross. I fed him and changed him, lied to the welfare and stole to get him clothes.'

The darkness made Kate super-sensitive to the rising tension in his body and voice and she closed her hand around his strong wrist, anchoring him to her warmth as she realised what must be coming. 'Only I couldn't be there all the time,' he said thickly, 'and when he was four he got sick and my mother was too high to notice anything wrong. By the time I got home from school it was too late; he had a big rash that turned out to be meningococcal disease. He died the next morning.'

Kate felt the first tremor and rolled over, wrapping him in her arms as he buried his face in her hair.

'God, Kate, it happened so fast.' She felt the wetness on her neck, the echo of agonised bewilderment in his voice. 'One day he was there, the next he was gone as if he'd never existed. Just like my father. Just like my mother when she killed herself six months later. Ross had had one chance for life, and that was me, and I wasn't there for him. I was his surrogate father and I let him die. Do you wonder that I couldn't cope with the thought of being responsible for another child?'

Kate held him in her arms as he silently wept, whispering her love in her heart, and perhaps, in her effort to give him solace, she might even have whispered it into the dark hair that brushed against her cheek as he bowed his head on her breast. It was no time to point out that Ross might have died anyway, that meningococcal was a fast and ruthless killer that even medical personnel sometimes failed to recognise in time.

In his mind he knew that but his heart still harboured that

thirteen-year-old's bitter grief. Drake had taken the guilt upon himself and it had petrified over time into a stony barrier to love, pushing out anything that might threaten to make him revisit that traumatic sense of loss.

Kate didn't know whether the night was cathartic for Drake, for he was already up and working when she woke the next morning, but for her it made her next action essential.

There was one thing they hadn't ever touched on in the past few weeks, and that was their first, cataclysmic coming together upstairs in his bedroom, when Drake had violated his most fundamental rule.

Just once.

Perhaps Drake still didn't realise his inexplicable oversight, or had forgotten or blocked it from his mind, but for Kate the lapse had begun to loom increasingly large in her thinking. And now it had assumed a critical significance.

Which was why she sloped off to Whitianga under the guise of a shopping trip, to re-visit the doctor. She still had not had a period, and this time she was leaving nothing to chance. At the risk of making a fool of herself she was going to get herself thoroughly checked out.

Just once.

Just once without a condom or any other form of contraception. What were the chances for a woman whose overstressed body had already stopped menstruating? she lectured herself on the road. Minuscule. At best. She had turned out not to be pregnant last time, and this time would be no different.

Just once.

Just once she would like to feel that she wasn't at the mercy of some malicious fate that took delight in ransacking her life.

Just once.

Yes, the doctor agreed cheerfully as she handed over a

prescription for prenatal vitamins. It only took once. That was why there were so many teenage pregnancies.

'At least that gives you an exact date to work with—some women like that because it helps give them ideas for the baby's name,' she told Kate briskly, obviously not sure whether to be amused or sympathetic at her patient's shell-shocked reception of the news. 'You're only four weeks along so it's early days yet, but there's no reason to think that this pregnancy won't progress normally. You must be pleased after what happened last time—you did say that the baby was very much wanted.'

Kate looked at her blankly and burst into tears.

Many tissues and much embarrassment later Kate slunk out of the clinic, congratulations ringing in her ears. Still in a daze she drove into the centre of town, hardly even aware of the light bustle of lunch-time traffic, and did the shopping that would provide the excuse for her trip. All in a strange state of suspended emotion.

Fortunately, when she arrived back and used her front door key to sneak in, it was to discover a note from Drake to say he'd received a reminder to take Prince for his annual vaccination, so she was relieved to find herself with some valuable breathing space. Time to calm down and recover her composure.

She carried her shopping bags into her bedroom and put them on the bed, frowning at the unexpected profusion. Had she really bought so much?

Koshka, whom she had found squeaking at the front door, prowled in and jumped up on the cream bedspread to nose into the interesting crackle of a brown paper bag.

'Oh, you want to have a look, do you?' Kate up-ended the bag and showed the cat the pale lemon-and-white striped top and leggings and the knitted hat that went with it. 'That's because we don't know whether it's a girl or a boy,' she said, carefully folding up the tiny outfit, size 0000, and putting it aside to dive into another bag. 'But I do have one or two pinks and a few blues…'

Soon the bed was awash with baby clothes and Koshka was lying down with her tail thumping back and forth on the bedspread looking mightily bored with the colourful array. Unable to resist, Kate pulled a cute little bobble hat over the velvety black ears and laughed at the squeak of offended feline dignity. She began to feel it…that long, slow, fizz deep inside, the inner fuse that was about to release an explosion of feelings.

'I suppose I did go a bit mad,' said Kate, whisking off the hat as the cat rolled over on its back. 'A lot mad,' she corrected herself, stacking everything into piles. She fetched an empty suitcase from the bottom of the walk-in wardrobe and unzipped it on the bed. 'Totally insane, in fact.'

'Kate?' The call coincided with a door slamming somewhere in the house, and by the click of claws on the kitchen tile.

Kate gasped in horror. Quickly she scooped up everything on the bed and stuffed it into the suitcase, slamming the lid shut and turning her back on it, just as Drake burst into the room.

His eyes immediately went to the suitcase. 'What's that? What are you doing?' he said hoarsely.

'Nothing,' she said quickly, for fear he would try to look.

His eyes flashed back to her face, seeing the lie. 'Packing your bags? You're leaving, Kate?'

'I—'

'Leaving me? Just like that? No discussion…no right of reply?' he said savagely. 'What were you going to do, prop a Dear Drake letter on my desk?'

'No—'

'How could you? After last night? After what I told you?'

His face changed, went as flat as his eyes, his beautiful voice: 'Or is that it? Are you afraid I might have inherited my mother's mental instability?'

'*No*—'

'Or my father's sheer, cold-blooded inhumanity?'

'No, Drake, it's nothing like that.'

He grabbed her hands and pulled her away from the bed to face him. 'Then tell me. What is it? What have I done wrong?'

She sighed. 'Nothing. You haven't done anything.'

Her sigh seemed to alarm him more than anything else. He laced his fingers through hers, securing her more completely to his cause.

'Don't go. Whatever it is, Kate, don't leave me,' he said, sending a piercing arrow of sweetness through her heart. She had never heard him plead before. Even last night, raw and bleeding with emotion, he had not spoken with such fierce desperation. 'Talk to me. Please. Just tell me what I can do to stop you. I've let you know the worst of me, but you can't judge me solely on what I've been. I can change, Kate…haven't these past few weeks shown you that? I let you into my life; don't turn around now and shut me out of yours! You can tell me anything. What is it you think I can't handle to hear?'

'That I love you, for one thing,' she said, taking her heart in both hands.

He looked stricken. 'I know. You told me that last night. But that's not the only thing, is it?'

It was her turn to be stricken. 'You know? *That's* all you have to say?'

His fingers tightened on hers as if he feared she was going to snatch them away. 'I'm not good with words—'

Her eyes widened. 'Drake—you're a *writer*.'

A muscle flickered along his jaw at her gentle scorn. 'I mean at *saying* them…to you. Other people don't matter.'

His discomfort made her heart stutter, then soar. 'You're also famous for your wit.'

'Wit is a weapon. Love is… It's dangerous… loving people,' he said, twining and re-twining their fingers.

'I know, but sometimes you have to do it anyway.'

He hunched his shoulders, his face flushing. 'For God's sake, Kate, you must know well enough by now I love you,' he admitted roughly. 'I told you I won't want any woman but you, and I've practically been doing handstands to impress you all month. You're the only woman I've ever wanted to have permanently in my life, to live with. You like it down here at Oyster Beach, don't you? We could move here together, you could freelance and I could write, we could be free—you and me…'

'And baby makes three,' she murmured, expecting the inevitable recoil.

He looked down into her upturned face. 'Are you saying that you won't marry me if I don't give you children?'

'I— *Marry?*'

'That's what people who love and trust each other do, don't they?'

'I—I didn't think you were the marrying kind,' she stammered.

'You've been wrong about me before. Don't you trust me to love and to cherish you for better and for worse? Why were you seeing the doctor again today, Kate?'

Her eyes dilated. 'You saw me?'

He shook his head. 'Ken's receptionist. You're living in a small town, sweetheart. Why didn't you tell me you were going? Was it too private?'

She tried to escape his hold, but he wouldn't let her go.

'Don't be frightened to tell me. Are you pregnant, Kate?'
She sucked in her breath. 'What makes you say that?'

'Because I was naked inside you that time you cried in
my arms. My first time being with a woman like that,' he
admitted, sensuously stroking her cheek and tracing his
finger around to the sensitive nerves behind her ear. 'I
forgot myself, until I was inside you, but I liked it far too
much to pull out. I never knew it would be so intense. I felt
myself come uncontrollably inside you and I loved it, but
I knew you weren't on the pill and after what you had just
gone through I knew I had to look after you. I've been
counting the days and you haven't had your period since.
And you glow, Kate…you don't see it but you *shine*, from
the inside out…'

She was confused by his pride, his deep satisfaction. 'I—
I thought you said you didn't want children.'

'That's because I didn't know what a powerful healer love
is… Yes, I'm afraid of the huge responsibility, the mistakes I
might make, but with you beside me, to share the worries and
the burdens as well as the rewards…you make me feel strong,
Kate. You give me faith in myself that I never had before.

'Unless…' he faltered, looking very un-Drakelike in his
uncertainty '…unless you're worried because you think I
might not be able to commit to being a good father… I don't
have a very good role model, or track record in the commitment department, do I?'

'Nor do I, come to that,' said Kate. 'And you told me you
thought *I* would still be a good mother. As soon as I get my
refund from my landlord I'll buy you a whole library of books
on how to be a good father,' she attempted to tease him back
into his usual arrogance.

He looked at the ceiling. 'Actually, you won't be getting

much of a refund, because your landlord thinks you and your cat have been shamelessly sponging off him all along.'

She looked at him uncomprehendingly, then the light dawned.

'*You* own the house next door?'

'I own several houses in Oyster Beach.'

'You knew that I was coming?' she accused.

'I knew the place was rented, but I don't keep up with the details. I didn't know until you arrived who the tenant was. I was angry at first, but only because you make me feel too deeply—you always have. I found myself wanting you too much. But once you were here…well—' he gave her a devilish grin of triumph '—it was just too good an opportunity to miss.'

'You could have had me thrown out at any time,' she said wonderingly.

'You had a water-tight rental agreement,' he said glibly 'And…uh…speaking of water.'

'The bore pump was never broken?' she guessed.

'A fifty-cent seal and it'll be good as new,' he said without an iota of regret.

'*You*—' she jabbed him in the chest '—are a very devious man…'

'Then it's just as well that I'm marrying a very shrewd and managing woman, isn't it?' he said, winding a lock of her hair around his finger and gently tugging her into his kiss. He nudged her knees back against the bed, his mouth slanting on hers, his tongue sliding against hers, his hands spanning her hips, stroking the stomach that harboured his baby, rising to cup the breasts that were designed for nurture and pleasure, only to freeze in mid-caress as he turned his head.

'What's that?'

'What?'

'That squeaking. In the suitcase.' He gave her an incredulous look. 'Don't tell me you were even going to pack the cat.'

'Oh. *Oh!*' She must have gathered Koshka up with the baby clothes. Her hand hovered uncertainly as she remembered the embarrassment of riches within, but Drake beat her to it, throwing back the lid and watching Koshka's head pop out of her cosy nest of clothes. He picked a white bootee off the lashing black tail.

'I've been shopping,' she said weakly, smoothing over the rest of the contents as the cat leapt from the case and shot out the door.

'So I see.' Drake fitted the tiny bootee over the tip of his thumb and waggled it at her. 'For our daughter?' he asked softly.

'Or our son.' She looked at his grave face, misty with memory, wistful for all the love that was yet to come. 'We could call him Ross, if you liked...' she offered, her eyes stinging with tears.

He slid his arm around her waist and tumbled her with him to the bed to kiss away her sorrow and replace it with laughter and love.

'And if it's a girl we can call her Joy, after you. Because that's what you bring me, sweetheart.' He made it a kiss and a vow. 'Joy for now and for always.'

Silhouette® Desire

NEW YORK TIMES BESTSELLING AUTHOR

DIANA PALMER

A brand-new Long, Tall Texans novel

IRON COWBOY

*Available March 2008
wherever you buy books.*

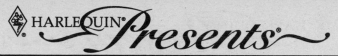

QUEENS of ROMANCE

The world's favorite romance writers

New and original novels you'll treasure forever from internationally bestselling Presents authors, such as:

Lynne Graham
Lucy Monroe
Penny Jordan
Miranda Lee

and many more.

Don't miss
THE GUARDIAN'S FORBIDDEN MISTRESS
by Miranda Lee
Book #2701

Look out for more titles from your favorite
Queens of Romance, coming soon!

www.eHarlequin.com

HP12701